PLAY

HOLLY S ROBERTS

WICKED STORY TELLING

Contents

ROMANCE TITLES

Completion Sports

Play

Goal

Strike

Kick

Ruck

Slam

Hotter Than Hell

Heat

Sizzle

Burn

Street Justice

Ignite

Combust

CHAPTER ONE

MY TEETH GROUND TOGETHER in something far worse than frustration. I couldn't believe I let her talk me into coming to this party. My sister, I mean, really? My sister!

I watched as she physically entertained a professional football team: half-naked, drunk, behaving like she had not a single inhibition. Not that she did, especially when she was drinking. I couldn't care less if she wanted to behave this way, but I did not want to be around to see it. I looked away; my eyes needed disinfectant. No one should see their older sister having her nipples sucked. After a certain age, no one should see their sister's nipples, period!

The party was in full swing, football players at the end of downtime blowing off pre-season steam. The room had plenty of women, drunk and rowdy, enjoying the celebration. It was everything but an all-out gang bang. At least so far.

I found the suite's small kitchen to hide while I tried to think of a way out that included taking my sister with me. It wasn't the best spot, because it opened on both sides; but at the moment, it was empty of partiers and sex-crazed athletes with their willing harems.

A noise behind me made me spin around.

"Heys, babes." The low, drunken voice slurred, casting obnoxious alcohol breath from four feet away. He took a single step forward with his long legs, and his ham-hock hand unexpectedly landed on my shoulder.

I twisted back and rammed my hip into the counter, forcing a grimace of pain from my lips.

What the hell?

He lifted me beneath my arms and turned me so my back was to the same counter. His arms then pinned me in as he brought his mouth down to mine. I turned my head at the last moment, and his wet lips went to my neck.

I placed my hands between us and pushed, which did absolutely nothing.

Shit!

I tried to scramble from his hold, but he was immovable. His alcohol-laden breath was too much, and bile rose in my throat. I was going to vomit.

His hand went into my hair, and he mumbled something. I jerked away hard, causing what felt like half my hair to tear out.

"Don't be thataway," he slurred as he tried to find my lips again.

He kept hold of a chunk of my hair, which made escape nearly impossible. I jammed my elbow into his side and started to scream. As the shriek worked its way from my throat, more of my hair tore out by the roots, and he staggered a foot back.

I pushed harder, and he released my hair. I twisted and tried to escape the kitchen but didn't realize his foot was in the way. I landed on my hands and knees, which was not a good thing in my current situation.

He stumbled as he tried to lift me to my feet, but I didn't want his hands on me and scrambled back.

"Leave the lady alone, Stump." The unidentified voice was gravellier than—my mind zeroed in on the name. Really? Stump?

Even at a time like this, my morbid sense of humor got the best of me, and I fought a full-out laugh. The football player causing all the trouble was a tree trunk. Stump did not fit in the slightest. My laugh was giddy with relief.

"What the fuck, Mac? I just wanted a kiss."

As the half-slurred conversation ensued, I went to my knees, placed my hands behind me, and then crab-walked backward away from both men. My palm hit something slippery, and I landed on my ass. The short skirt I wore had ridden up my thighs, and my lacy underwear was on full display.

I'd worn the clothes at my sister's insistence. Now I showed a totally undignified amount of flesh, and heat rose up my neck into my cheeks.

"She doesn't seem to want your kiss," the man ground out. "I'm about to bruise my throwing arm planting my fist in your face," he continued. His voice didn't rise, but the forceful, tightly controlled words revealed anger.

"The scunt owes me one kiss," the asshole said.

Stump literally went airborne. He landed with a thud against the tile. An "Oomph" followed when the other man landed on top of him.

How many football players can you get in a compact kitchen?

I found out when multiple legs, not caring that they trampled me, piled in from two directions. Even with numerous sets of bulging arms, they struggled to hold my irate savior back once they had him on his feet.

"He's drunk, Mac. Let it go," one of them shouted.

"All's good. She's okay," said another one.

At this point, a zillion sets of eyes turned to me. I looked up, blinked twice, swallowed, and saw the god of football, the man who had come to my rescue stood before me.

Killian MacGregor, The Mac, or Mac the Knife, as fans called him because of his throwing arm, was staring. At me, and my baby blue lacy panties. Maybe I could have saved some of my humiliation by trying to peel the skirt down, but no. I gaped at six and a half feet of boiling testosterone. Broad strokes made his face a work of art, heavy eyebrows, dark pools for eyes, high cheekbones, and his jaw, almost too perfectly square with full lips displaying a not-so-pleased scowl. My eyes traveled from his corded neck to his black t-shirt, which looked painted over each straining muscle. Those muscles were restrained by two teammates. Jeans encased his long legs all the way to his black leather boots. My eyes, with a will of their own, traveled back up to see him shake the guys off like ants. He elbowed his teammates aside and scooped me off the floor like I weighed nothing. Yes, I was thin, but at just under six feet, I wasn't small. For the first time in my life, I felt like Tinker Bell.

My brain did a backflip.

Killian MacGregor saw me scrambling like a clown on a kitchen floor in my all but bare glory. Oh, god, please just strike me dead.

He let my feet stabilize but held onto me with a secure grip. His hold made me feel safe and I leaned into him while I tried getting my legs to support me. His head dipped and warm tequila breath feathered across my cheek. It had the exact opposite effect that his teammates breath had on me and I felt lightheaded.

"Are you okay?" He rearranged my skirt without taking his eyes from mine.

"Uhm." No words came out. His hand, running across my hip and ass, made me suck in air.

It wasn't just the tequila I smelled.

Musky, salty, man was sinking my IQ level to my shoe size. I couldn't get a word out of my suddenly closed-off lungs and heat pooled low in my belly.

"Come on, let's check you out."

And did I mention, when not angry, his voice was smooth velvet?

He didn't give me a chance to respond; his hand wrapped around mine, and I mean wrapped. There was nothing left of my fingers. He used his body to block me from the other guys and backed me up slightly before turning me around so I preceded him through a short hallway. His small touch to my shoulder guided me in the direction he wanted. He gave a gentle backward pull on my hand, so I stopped. Reaching in front of me, he opened the door, ushering me into a gargantuan bathroom.

The party suite was located in one of the most exclusive hotels in Phoenix, and if the incredible front room didn't give it away, this one did. Large gold fixtures and marble countertops made every detail luxurious. My tiny apartment bedroom would fit in here.

The door gave a soft thud and then he turned and locked us in. He followed my nervous gaze as I glanced at the bolted door. Yes, he saved me, but I'd just had a bad experience and it might not be a good idea to be locked in a room with another drunk jock.

Reading my mind, his low voice assured me, "The lock is to keep them out. You can leave anytime you want. Now, up you go."

He lifted me so my ass landed on the cold marble. Involuntarily, my hands went onto his shoulders. I blinked in the stark light of the room, suddenly realizing my hair must be a scary mess. Like Medusa hair with the most gorgeous man on the planet.

I turned toward the mirror and managed to fight back a hysterical scream.

Medusa had an ugly sister.

Before I could bring my hands up, his were there, smoothing down the messy tangles. Oh. My. God. I, the connoisseur of male arms, drizzled into a puddle of lust as his sculpted biceps took over my peripheral vision, causing me to wobble backward toward the mirror. At that moment, I had absolutely no control. Did I pant?

Oh God, what if I was turning into my sister?

His powerful arms steadied me. "Did you hit your head?" Concern deepened his voice and his long fingers moved to my scalp, running over the contours, checking for bumps.

I'd yet to utter more than a semi-coherent grunt. My shaking fingers reached for his forearms.

Pure, hot, steel.

I sucked in air, trying to speak. "I'm fi fine." Shit, if I could only articulate a single sentence.

I stopped breathing when his gaze returned to mine.

He released my head, lowering his hands to rest on the counter beside my hips, his nose an inch away. "Sorry about Stump." His breath whispered across my lips. "He's usually pretty tame, at least when not drinking. I'm Killian." His eyes quickly dipped below my neck but came immediately back up. "And you are?"

I wondered how badly my shirt gaped open. Not much to see, but his irises had expanded at the quick glance or maybe it was him adjusting to the light. I tried to speak, realized my mouth was hanging open, and snapped it shut.

Damn, I bit my tongue.

"Owww." My head involuntarily went forward and my forehead cracked against his nose.

"Whoa, it's all right. I'm sorry." He moved back, his hands coming up in a defensive motion.

He thought I was angry about him checking out my practically non-existent chest. My life couldn't get worse. Medusa hair, mono-syllable communication, bloody tongue, and I'd banged the Scorpions' star football player in the nose. It was time for me to melt onto the floor. Someone needed to throw water and get the process started.

"I, I bwit my tongue." I said as a way to apologize

He rubbed his nose and checked for blood. There was none, which was maybe the only thing I could be thankful for. The corners of his lips tilted upward.

"Let's try this again." He extended his hand. "I'm Killian."

My fingers rose. "I'm Webecca Re...becca." Damn, no water splashed me. Where was Dorothy when I needed her?

He grasped my hand. The small tilt to his lips went into a full-blown grin and fuck, I kid you not, dimples.

Jacob Elordi who?

The man I was currently fixated on was the sexiest man alive.

"Nice to meet you, Webecca." His dimples hollowed farther.

I circled my tongue inside my mouth trying to get feeling back. His eyes followed the movement. I licked my lips like the complete needy woman I was turning into and god, he looked like he wanted to devour me. His gaze shifted to my neck, my chest, belly, and then slowly down my legs. With leisurely concentration, his gaze traveled back up. He hadn't released my hand and he moved in close, using his hips to spread my knees.

Anxiety took over. "I ne need to go." I'd made a big enough fool of myself already. I couldn't handle Killian MacGregor and I knew it.

My fingers slipped from his grasp while every rough callus on his hand caused shivers to trail up my arms.

He sighed roughly, giving me a slight look of disappointment, but backed away. "I'll walk you out. Did you come with someone?"

"My, umm, my sister." Two semesters from graduating with a bachelor's in medical laboratory science and I came across as a complete dunce.

"Then let's go find your sister." His fingers tightened on my hips, and I found myself standing again. The heat in my lower belly ignited again.

His dimples had disappeared, and for the first time, I managed a stable sentence, "Thank you for what you did."

His eyes turned guarded. "Stump could get in a lot of fucking trouble from the coach. Or you could even press charges. There is no excuse for what he did."

I stood there in shock. Stump, obviously his teammate, had tried to kiss me at a party where a lot more than kissing was going on. My sister would have had sex with him there in the kitchen. I was a woman who believed no meant no, but the last thing I wanted was to draw more attention to myself and why I was at the party.

I shook my head slightly. "No, I'm fine. I'm sorry to have taken your time." I couldn't look at him anymore. I turned and tried to grab for the door handle. He leaned around me and unsnapped the lock, then opened the door.

His lips practically touched my ear. "The pleasure was mine."

I escaped from the enclosed space with Killian, in search of my traitorous sister. She probably had no idea I was in trouble and she would simply laugh at what had happened. Killing her after I got her home was an option.

Killian didn't touch me, just stayed close enough that I felt the heat from his towering body. Curious eyes followed our movement. Men, some football players, some obviously not, and women who dressed in scanty clothing gave the party the exact vibe it was going for. I should have turned around and left as soon as I saw what was happening. No wonder Stump thought he had a kiss coming. I searched for Candi. Yep, a name fit for this exact circumstance; given at birth by our parents. She'd tried to live up to the name since she was fifteen. Mine, Rebecca; good, plain, old-fashioned, Rebecca. The responsible one. The one with extremely un-comfortable lacy underwear that Killian MacGregor and half his team had seen.

My eyes scanned the room and I tried to avoid naked breasts even though they might be my sisters. She wasn't in the front room, kitchen, or dining area. No Candi.

The bedrooms.

Damn. I couldn't look there. No way.

"She's not here," I said, trying not to panic.

I turned and glanced up at Killian. His eyes betrayed the fact that he knew exactly where my sister was.

"Did you drive?" he asked.

"I'm the DD. It's my sister's car and she drove here and kept the keys." I should have taken them as soon as we arrived, but no, it was one more stupid thing to add to tonight's long list.

"I'll take you home," he said casually, though I wasn't sure his eyes appeared happy.

"No. I mean thank you, but I'll call a cab."

He ran his hand through his hair, not brown, not blonde, but soft, mouthwatering sable. "I haven't had a drink in over an hour and then it was only one shot. After what happened, I'm seeing you home."

It was a statement. Final, absolute, no arguing back.

I exhaled slowly and gave in. "Thank you."

Chapter Two

Killian took my hand. Cripes, this man liked to touch. He escorted me out of the suite and then the hotel. A valet brought his car around. Not what I expected. No flashy sports car, but a BMW. He opened the door for me and I sank into the blissful leather.

"Buckle up." His hand was already pulling the strap across my chest and sliding it effortlessly into the clasp next to my hip.

I gulped and prayed the sound was silent. Killian Mac-Gregor was taking me home to my semi-rundown apartment building, a mile from the state college. I took another long breath trying to slow my heart rate. It didn't help. The car smelled just like him. Someone could bottle this and make a fortune.

"Where to?" he asked with one confident hand on the steering wheel.

"The university." At least it didn't come out breathless.

He was a shadow in the dark interior, but I felt his eyes on me. His head dipped slightly and I had the craziest feeling he was staring at my legs.

A moment later he asked, "Dancer?"

"Runner."

He didn't comment, just pulled around the long circular drive and headed out to the main road. The campus was twenty minutes away without traffic, and for once I wished there was a mile-long pileup. I wanted to breathe in his scent for the rest of the night. Maybe the rest of my life because a girl deserved to dream. Sable-haired babies; tall, coordinated athletes. We'd make the perfect children if they looked like their father. A laugh escaped my lips. Crazy. I was absolutely certifiable.

"Do you want to share the joke?" he asked.

In the close confines of the car, his thick, molasses voice made me fidget. My good-girl sense of honor got the best of me and I spilled part of the beans. "This is unreal. I'm sorry, I don't want to make you uncomfortable, but really. You, Killian MacGregor, driving me home."

He gave a low, sexy chuckle. "My mother would be proud."

"Oh gosh, you even have a mother."

This time he laughed long and hard. Every nerve ending I possessed sizzled and my breathing grew shallow again.

"Yes, and I was even created the old-fashioned way," he replied when his laughter died.

He. Did. Not. Just. Say. That.

His next words drew me out of the fantasy.

"How old are you?"

I turned and looked at his profile. The line of his jaw and curve of his nose where still perfect even in shadow.

"Twenty-one and old enough to know better than to let my sister drag me to a party like the one we just left. Sorry, no disrespect, but that's not my scene."

I had completely blown it now. Given away the fact that "easy college girl" wasn't my thing even if, for the first time in my life, I wanted to qualify for the slut Olympics. I couldn't help thinking about what he saw. My favorite skirt, a tad too short, but it accented my legs, which were by far my best feature. Unfortunately, when it came to my chest, there was nothing much to show. I'd worn a peach-col- ored, button-up blouse with just a touch of lace on the shoulders for sleeves; more clothes than any two girls at the party wore, including my sister. I refused to think about the panties. My nothing-special brown hair had been curled but was now in complete disarray. I was tall and gangly looking, though he had no idea I was usually quite coordinated and lithe. Well, maybe he did. He asked if I was a dancer.

He glanced at me and the headlights from an oncoming car showed that sexy tilt to his lips.

"Do you run for the college team?" He turned his head back to the road.

"Yes. Scholarship." I wasn't ashamed.

"So, you're good?"

Well, maybe I was ashamed. "Middle of the pack."

He didn't say anything after that. I gave directions when we got closer. He pulled in front of the dilapidated college dorm apartments and my hand went to the door handle.

"Do not touch that." There it was again, his "do what I say" voice.

Funny, because I didn't even consider going against the order.

"I'm sorry as fuck about tonight," he said, surprising me.

He turned his head my way but remained completely in shadow. I could still picture every gorgeous line on his face.

My heart thumped so loud he should be able to hear it. "I'm okay. No harm, no foul," I told him.

His deep, throaty chuckle was back. "You a baseball fan?"

"Not really." I ran track, but wasn't much for any sport, and didn't they have fouls in football?

"Football?"

"No."

"But you came to a football party?"

I would dream of his voice tonight. "My mistake but thank you for your help."

"You made the party," he hesitated, "interesting. I watched you all night. I don't suppose you'll come to another one?"

He'd watched me!

"You suppose right," I said. I would give anything to stop the chit-chat and slide into the back seat with him. Why was I pushing him away?

"You attached?"

"Attached?" Did I really need to repeat everything he said?

"Significant other?" I heard the laughter in his voice again and knew his dimples flashed. "Boyfriend?"

"Uh, no."

"I'll walk you inside." He stepped out before I could protest.

My door opened and his hand took hold of my forearm and then slid down to my hand. I couldn't remember the last time I held hands with a guy. Grade school maybe. I entered the security code at the lobby entrance and turned to say goodnight.

"To your door." Again, no room for argument, and I scurried along like a trained puppy straight to my apartment door.

I should stand up to him and tell him he was pushy, but that wasn't me. My wimpy persona was exactly why I let my sister force me into going to the party.

"Key." The hand not holding mine came out.

I dutifully placed the key in his palm and watched his large, deft fingers unlock my door.

He looked up.

I failed to breathe.

His incredibly full, sensuous lips leaned in and he kissed my forehead. I mean really. My forehead and placed the keys in my hand.

"Goodnight, Webecca."

I couldn't get any words out and turned and walked inside.

"And, Legs," he said.

I peered over my shoulder.

"If you do come to another party, say hello."

I nodded then shut and locked the door behind me.

Holy fucking shit. The dream father of my future children just walked away and I knew I'd never see him again. But I would fantasize and dream about him for at least ten years.

Killian MacGregor's warm lips had touched my forehead and I was a goner.

CHAPTER THREE

T HE ENTIRE WEEK AFTER the party, I spent every available minute on the internet researching Killian Macgregor like some obsessed fan. I couldn't seem to help myself.

Twenty-five years old, star quarterback in college and first-round draft pick when he turned pro at twenty-one. Two years ago, he took over the starting quarterback position for the Scorpions. He instantly became one of the country's most eligible bachelors. But, as always, there was a downside. Killian had a quick temper, used his fists when push came to shove, and for a non-thug position like quarterback, he had a thug reputation. I'd seen that quick temper in action. And I couldn't forget, he had the face of an angel.

I dug deeper. His single mom raised him along with one brother, but no other articles gave insight into his family. An in-depth feature about his high school years shed some light on his temper. He grew up in a poor area and attended a rough high school. He learned to use his fists until his throwing arm caught the eye of the varsity football coach his sophomore year. His teammates had his back after that. An early picture showed a big, cocky kid, surrounded by five huge teammates. It was the same angel face without the refinement it showed now. The boys all sneered with their arms strung across each other's shoulders.

Killian MacGregor was a bad boy.

What every girl wanted. But not me. At least not until Killian MacGregor held my hand and then kissed my forehead when he said goodbye.

I couldn't get him out of my mind, so I did what I always did. I ran. Albeit early in the mornings because the desert heat tried to melt my body to the concrete, but I ran, nonetheless.

I slipped on running shorts over my shear-blue bikini panties minus itchy lace, followed by a form-fitting sports bra and a white tank top. My socks and favorite running shoes came next. I secured my hair in a tight ponytail, jumped on my toes a few times, circled my arms, and set off at a leisurely pace for about a mile. I then stopped and stretched my warmed muscles for ten minutes. It was now time for the real part of my run. The endorphin high kicked into my bloodstream on the fifth mile.

Legs, he'd called me Legs.

I continued running until all thought focused on my next step. At twelve miles, I reached a point where nothing mattered. Not the scenery, temperature, or Killian memories, and I kept going. Eventually, I hit the last low-angled hill, which took me back to my apartment.

It didn't matter how many miles I ran; I still didn't get a good night's sleep that night or the next.

Two weeks after the party, I wore out my track shoes and bought a new pair. I hit the pavement hard. Three weeks and I stopped watching television news, reading articles on my phone, or even listening to gossip about Killian or his team. I needed sleep, food, and a shrink; the order was optional. I acted like a lovesick groupie and it had to stop.

I still hadn't forgiven my sister, but per in her usual demeanor, my anger didn't bother her in the least. I was her boring sister and no fun to hang out with. She told me I was a complete stick in the mud. She'd asked if I saw the girl at the party who came between Stump and Killian. She had no idea it was me, and I wasn't going to tell her. She didn't even apologize for not being around to give me a ride home.

I applied myself to my end of summer classes and prepared for spring track season. Ignoring the fact that professional football was gearing up for its first pre-season game, I refused to think about Killian MacGregor. Well almost. I thought of him as soon as the lights went out each night and still dreamed about what our babies would look like. Pathetic. That was me.

Regular classes began in August along with twice-weekly practice overseen by the college running coach. My fantasy world, or trying to get past it, had me ready for everything the coach threw my way.

Still no possibility of me winning at this level, but my time was faster than it had ever been.

It sucked because in high school I was the star, the tall running giant. Entering the college arena put my Olympic dreams into perspective. I, Rebecca Lesley Cavanaugh, was middle of the pack; nothing special in the world of long-distance runners. On the bright side, many runners didn't hit their full stride until their thirties. Still, by then I'd be completely into my future career, running simply to stay in shape, and not looking back. I'd given up on my dream long ago and moved on. If only I could do the same thing about my dream man.

My class load was heavy, but I still managed two dates, arranged by my best friend, Amanda. Both times the men and I didn't quite meet eye to eye. I was an inch or two taller even though I wore flat shoes. My head tilted slightly downward to speak and I hunched my shoulders when I walked beside them. The last thing I felt was small. Obviously, like my previous dates, my height intimidated men. I knew Amanda gave the guys fair warning, but seeing me in person, even in flat shoes, was a lot more sobering. I'd even taken more than my normal time to get ready for the first date. A little eyeliner to make my blue eyes stand out, a touch of blush to liven my tanned cheeks, and my favorite date outfit.

The second man didn't get so lucky, because I didn't bother with the extra makeup or putting on my favorite skirt and blouse. Not that skirt, I might never wear that one again. My lack of preparation didn't mattered because my thirty-something-year-old second date couldn't get past my tall frame and my ordinary, non-super-model looks. Life sucked, and I compared every man to Killian MacGregor.

I went back to concentrating on college.

The multi-leveled, stadium-styled classroom held more than two hundred students. I sat in the fourth row, dead center, taking notes and trying to stay awake throughout the lecture. The side door opened and a man walked toward the professor. Doctor Lanovitch didn't bother turning off the microphone when the man spoke.

"I have a special delivery." The voice resounded through the room as he showed a medium-sized envelope to the professor.

He now had the attention of the entire class.

The instructor's eyes skimmed us students, landed on me, and said right into the microphone, "Miss Cavanaugh."

Oh shit.

I stood slowly, squeezed behind the seats of my fellow row mates, and then walked down the side stairs toward the man interrupting the class. He held out the envelope and after I tentatively took it, he turned and walked out the same door he'd entered.

The professor's eyebrows shot up before I looked down. Rebecca Cavanaugh was handwritten in a bold scrawl on the front. I muttered an apology, not looking up, and returned to my seat. The lecture resumed and I tried hard to focus but my eyes kept returning to my name. I no longer had any problems staying awake, but at the same time, I didn't hear another word or take a single note.

After class, I walked into the one-hundred-and-ten-degree heat and zombied to the library. My ass hit a chair, I drank half my water bottle and went back to staring at the envelope in my hand. The fluttering in my chest had me longing for one thing, but I knew I was being an idiot. Killian MacGregor would never send me anything. I lifted the envelope, took a deep breath, and opened it slowly.

Three tickets slipped out along with a small slip of paper.

Legs,

Bring two friends.

K

I was too young for a heart attack, or so I thought. Yes, the outside heat left my body overly warm, hot even, but all the blood left my head and traveled who knew where. A wave of dizziness washed over me and I took a quick sip of water. I realized that wasn't helping, so I put my head between my knees.

This reaction, completely ridiculous, over the top and borderline psychotic. But it didn't matter. Killian sent me tickets to his first home, pre-season game. My hands trembled and I rapidly sucked in air, trying to get myself under control. I finally managed, barely, to sit up straight and re-read the slip of paper. The four words and one initial hadn't changed. I lifted the paper to my chest and held it there for countless minutes while I tried not to panic.

Fantasy was one thing, reality totally another. I, simple and plain Rebecca Cavanaugh, was not football god material. I liked the dream better. I checked the tickets again. This Sunday, the Phoenix Scorpions played in their first home game and I had three passes.

Chapter Four

Wнат the hell did you wear to a football game in an indoor arena anyway? And what did it matter? Killian probably wouldn't even see me or I him. I might just go, watch the game, and return to my apartment. I could go to bed early and dream without my nerves going crazy.

I called Amanda.

"Really, Becca, there's no dress code. Be comfortable, comfortable shoes and a lightweight top will do. The stadium's cooled, but still gets warm when all the hot bodies pile in."

"Okay, thanks."

I hadn't told Amanda or Lyle, my prerequisite black, gay friend, as he called himself, how I got the tickets, just that I had them and they were invited. Amanda was great in that she didn't ask too many questions, because her mind was currently filled with finding a student-teaching position. But she did enjoy football and went to all the college games. She also stood nine inches shorter than me and made me feel goliath. Lyle was two inches shorter than me, an arts major, and gay since before puberty. He really enjoyed football but only because of the sweaty players or so he said.

If I did happen to see Killian and he didn't like Lyle's lifestyle, that would be that. No more dreams. I had no room for homophobic macho athletes, even if they filled my late-night fantasies.

Amanda picked me up in her seven-year-old Honda Civic. Lyle already occupied the shotgun position, so I folded my tall frame into the back and turned slightly sideways to accommodate my legs. I wore my ocean-blue tight stretch capri pants that ended just below my knees. My top half was covered by a gray cropped t-shirt with a bright yellow Tweety Bird on the front. White deck shoes minus socks covered my feet. I had put my hair in a ponytail and propped large, dark sunglasses on my head for effect.

As we drew closer to the stadium, Lyle turned to me. "Let me see those tickets so we can try and park by the entrance we need."

I removed them from my small, cross-over-the-shoulder purse, and handed them forward.

A minute later, Lyle turned my way again. "Umm, who gave you these tickets?"

I looked into his questioning eyes. "Why? What's wrong with them?"

"They're for the VIP skybox."

"What?" Amanda and I asked at the same time.

Lyle gave me a look. "So, do I need to ask again or will you give up your sugar daddy?"

I laughed at the thought of Mac the Knife being any woman's sugar daddy. "Killian MacGregor sent them to me."

The silence lasted a full five seconds.

"What the hell?" Amanda swerved through two lanes of traffic and exited the freeway nowhere close to our turnoff. I breathed a sigh of relief that we survived her display of missile evasive maneuvers. Lyle, totally unaffected by our near brush with death, looked at me with something like horror on his face.

"What?" I asked with absolute innocence.

Amanda pulled into the first parking lot she came to, put the car in park, turned my way and glared. "How the hell do you know Killian MacGregor?"

Before I could answer, Lyle spoke slowly, "You mean Mac the Knife, starting quarterback for the Scorpions, Killian MacGregor?"

I kept the nonchalant look on my face even though I knew my cheeks were bright red. "That would be him. I met him at that party my sister took me to a while back."

"But, let me get this straight. I set you up on two dates and you've had Killian MacGregor on the hook?" Amanda sputtered.

I dropped my evasive act and gave a sigh. "Look, I received the tickets earlier this week, but it's the first time I've heard from him since the party. One of the players got a little out of line, Killian stepped in and I'm sure this is his way of making things right. I had no idea the tickets were for some skybox thing."

"Not just a skybox, the VIP skybox. And girlfriend, we're totally underdressed." Lyle glared at Tweety Bird. I knew it was the bird because he had no interest in my breasts.

I looked down at myself and sighed. "Look, guys, we don't have to go. I'll treat you both to pizza and make up for it."

Amanda pulled the car back onto the road. "Over my dead body. Killian MacGregor sends VIP tickets and we are damn well taking advantage of it. I can't believe you would seriously go out for pizza." The disgust in her voice came through loud and clear.

"If you don't want Mr. MacGregor, I'll take him," Lyle said with pure muscle worship in his voice. "That man gets more than just the juices flowing, if you know what I mean."

Thinking about Lyle's juices flowing was not a pleasant thought and I seriously didn't want to know what he was talking about.

"I doubt we'll even see him," I said calmly.

"Oh, baby girl, we'll see him. These tickets kind of seal that deal," Lyle practically purred.

I wanted to slap the smug look off his face. "Don't get your hopes up."

"It's my dick that will go up once I'm in the same room with him."

"Not a pretty picture, perv," Amanda said in a cheerful voice.

I wasn't wrong. This was Killian's way of setting things right. It was most likely a last-minute thought. It had to be.

We arrived at the stadium ten minutes later. By that time, doubt had set in. All week I'd dealt with the prospect of going to the game; enjoying time with my friends, watching a sport I knew nothing about, and getting a small peek at Killian. But I convinced myself I wouldn't be talking to him. Now, Lyle had my heart racing and my knees feeling weak. I was willing to admit the lack of circulation could be caused by the tight quarters in the backseat that scrunched up my legs, but I had my doubts.

Men waving flags directed us inside the stadium parking lot and to a row of quickly filling spaces. So much for parking near the entrance we needed.

"Let's get inside, out of the heat, and then we can walk around until we find our way to the skybox," Lyle said as he looped his arms around our shoulders and steered us to follow the rest of the crowd.

Most people wore purple and white, the team colors. Even Amanda sported a team jersey. Lyle looked halfway dignified in a form-fitting pair of jeans and an off-white, untucked short-sleeved linen shirt. Tweety Bird and I were out of place. We handed our tickets over at the turnstile.

"Wait right here, please." The woman immediately spoke into her portable radio while gesturing us to the side.

She ignored us after that, but a minute later an electric cart pulled up. "I'll take you to the elevator," the driver said.

Amanda squeezed my hand when we sat down. "You're sure you haven't seen him once these past two months?"

"I'm sure." It hadn't been two entire months. It was fifty-two days. Somehow my voice sounded normal, at least to my ears. I saw Killian MacGregor every night in my dreams.

The cart driver took us to an elevator and when we stepped off, a woman wearing a white blouse and black uniform pants checked our tickets. She didn't so much as raise an eyebrow when she said, "Right this way." We followed while staring at the luxury offered on this floor. It only proved I didn't belong.

The first thing I noticed were men dressed in suits. About a dozen people stood around talking inside the skybox, all looked like they were dining in an exclusive restaurant. One younger woman actually wore a skin-tight, sequined purple jersey that displayed her playboy breasts. Slowly, all eyes turned our direction, and it was obvious these people thought we had the wrong room. Cut that, wrong floor.

The lady with the night club jersey stepped forward, put her dainty, well-manicured hand out, cranked her head back to look me in the eye, and said, "You must be Rebecca. I'm Malory, Blitz's wife. Killian asked me to keep an eye out for you and your friends and make you feel at home."

"Tha, thank you," I stumbled. "Um, these are my friends Amanda and Lyle."

"Hi." Amanda the talker failed me with a one-word greeting.

"Hi, gorgeous, I'm Lyle."

Malory shook their hands and looked genuinely pleased to meet us. She leaned in close to me and conspiratorially whispered, "Don't let the big shots," she nodded at the suited gentlemen standing around us, "intimidate you. They're nothing but big fluffy puppy dogs when you get to know them."

I finally managed to exhale. I had hated Malory on sight because she was everything I wasn't: short, buxom, blonde, and absolutely stunning. But I could forgive her everything for making me and my friends feel welcome.

She introduced us to everyone, the team owner, his wife, and staff echelon. I stopped trying to remember names. Malory walked us to the bar, in the opposite corner from the door, told us to order whatever beverage we wanted, and to also order from the menu. Our food would be delivered. Two huge television screens took up the side walls. This was another world, but as awkward as I felt, what I really wanted was to stare down at the field and catch a glimpse of Killian.

"This is fucking unbelievable," Lyle whispered in my ear. "You've struck gold, baby girl."

I shot daggers of fire his way and as discreetly as I could and gave him a short painful nipple twist. Of course, he loved it and managed only a small gasp. Amanda was right, he was a huge perv, but every kinky thing I'd learned about sex came from his verbal sharing of escapades. Too bad, besides nipple twisting, I'd never been able to try them on anyone.

Chapter Five

MALORY DIRECTED US TO the front seats, which were to the right of the owner and his group but separated by an aisle.

"I'd rather sit in the back, if that's okay," I said.

"These are Killian's and he wants you sitting here," she said.

Just as we took the proffered seats, the crowd started clapping and cheering. Music blared and the lights dimmed. A spotlight showed down on the field and the announcer blared out over the music.

"Your Phoenix Scorpions," he said in a deep voice.

I saw Killian, helmet dangling from his hand, leading the team onto the field at a steady jog. The crowd went nuts.

Fucking hell.

In street clothes, he was a female wet dream, but in pads, the number twenty jersey, and skin-tight football pants, completely panty melting. Damp hair hung just a little below his ears and was plastered to his head. He made the wet shaggy style look scrumptious. I continued to subconsciously drool as he sat on the grass, spread his legs, and stretched.

"Heart attack here. Where's the medic?" Amanda said in a low voice.

Malory heard, laughed, and said too loudly, "We keep smelling salts on hand for just this purpose."

"I need some of those," Lyle said loudly.

I couldn't believe it when everyone laughed or at least grinned. Lyle always had that way about him. He was totally secure in his sexuality, even in a group of macho professional sports icons.

They played the national anthem and I didn't look at the flag once. My gaze stayed on Killian. Amanda elbowed me gently, but still, I didn't look away.

Killian walked to the middle of the field with two of his teammates and stood with the referee. The other team sent players too and they all shook hands. A coin was tossed and the other team gave high fives. I had no idea what it meant.

The game finally started. The other team kicked the ball while Killian stood on the sideline. He ran onto the field after a whistle blew. He threw two passes which his players missed. He then handed the ball off to a teammate on the next play. I knew this because Amanda and Lyle quietly explained everything going on. He made a short pass but the player missed the next one. Right before the Scorpions punted, Killian slow jogged to the sidelines and watched intently while the other team's quarterback did his thing.

Several plays later, the ball was punted again and Killian returned to the field.

Two handoffs, one pass, and on the next play, Killian threw a forty-yard touchdown. The fans went crazy. I leapt from my chair and cheered before noticing there was very little fanfare inside the box. Heat traveled to my cheeks, but Malory just laughed.

"This is pre-season and there will be a lot of player substitutions. Neither team will show their best stuff until the regular season starts."

While Malory talked, I turned my eyes to Killian. Players slapped him on the back as he walked to the sideline. About ten feet from the white line, he turned, looked up toward the skybox, and blew a kiss.

Holy shit.

"He's kinda into you if you haven't figured that out yet."
At least this time Malory managed to lean forward and
speak in a semi-low voice.

I intertwined my fingers and pulled them close to my
chest. They'd begun to tremble. I think Lyle and Amanda
were just as stunned as I was. I sat in contemplative silence, waiting for Killian to return to the field, but it never
happened. Malory explained that they didn't want to risk
injuring their star quarterback, and because the second and
third string quarterback positions were up for grabs, the
team wanted to check out its other options. I listened with
half an ear, never taking my eyes off Killian. He remained
focused the entire game, talked to the coach a few times,
encouraged players, and never looked back up at the skybox.

The Scorpions won thirty-five to fourteen.

I'd barely touched the finger foods we'd ordered and only
drank a bottle of water. I turned to Amanda and Lyle. "You
guys up for that pizza I promised you?"

Malory answered for them. "Killian told me to bring you
and your friends to the locker room. Eat some of this food
or order something else. We'll go down in about forty-five
minutes."

I looked at Lyle and Amanda and asked, "Are you guys good with that?"

Lyle's face showed deep concentration. "Let's see. Me in a locker room full of muscle-bound athletes? Chances of catching a few naked? I think I can handle the strain."

Malory looked at Lyle with a patient grin. "If I were you, I'd keep my eyes up. These are macho jocks after all."

"Gotcha, sister."

"I'm with Lyle," Amanda said. "There's no way on earth I'd miss this."

I was a nervous wreck and they were not helping. My stomach was a bundle of nerves, which kept me from eating.

Malory made small talk with Amanda and Lyle, casting curious looks my way now and then, but asked me few questions. The owner, his wife and his crew left five minutes after the game ended without saying goodbye to anyone. A few of the others left, while we continued to hang.

Finally, Malory told us to follow her and we trailed behind with the same wide eyes that we had when we entered the secret world of pro football. It took ten minutes to get to the underground locker room. As we approached,

I heard voices, laughter, the occasional shout and general camaraderie. Malory didn't check to see if everyone was decent, she just pushed through the door and started congratulating the players she came to.

My eyes circled the room looking for one person.

"Pure fucking eye candy coming from your right," Lyle whispered in my ear.

I turned and there he was. Freshly showered, tight black t-shirt molding his broad shoulders and muscled chest, tapering to a sleek waist, with black jeans accenting his long legs. I took it all in, unable to breathe. No picture on television or the internet did him justice.

His brown, melting eyes looked into mine. When he was close enough, he took my hand, leaned in, and kissed me on the forehead. "Thank you for coming."

His luscious scent almost knocked me over and I worried about passing out. I clenched my thighs and heat was simmering low in my belly again. Killian's hand sent an extra zing body, and like the last time I saw him, I stumbled for words. "Um, well thank you for inviting me, um, us, I mean." Yep, I had completely forgotten my best friends' names. Mac the Knife's lips were about six inches from mine and they looked better than my favorite dessert.

My best friend finally saved me. "Hi, Mr. MacGregor. I'm Amanda and this is Lyle."

I turned and gave her a relieved smile.

"Hi, Amanda. Please call me Killian." He switched my hand to his left one, tucked me loosely into his side, shook Amanda's hand, and then greeted Lyle. "Pleasure to meet you, Lyle."

I think Lyle was in just as much trouble as I was. His usual flirty, devil-may-care repertoire deserted him and he settled for a handshake followed by a choked, "Nice to meet you, too." Though he managed to say it without stumbling.

Killian pulled me even closer. "I was hoping I could take you all out to dinner if you don't have other plans."

Lyle's eyes lit up, but Amanda cut in. "Actually, I need to get back to campus and Lyle has rehearsal first thing in the morning."

This was news to me and it took about two seconds to realize Amanda was lying through her teeth. Lyle caught on just as quickly and declined, though his eyes showed genuine remorse.

"Another time then?" Killian gave them both his dimpled smile and I saw my friends melt just like I did.

"Yes, definitely. We'll hold you to that," Amanda said as she looked toward the door. "Will someone be able to show us out of here?"

"I'll have security escort you. Thanks for coming and I hope you had a good time."

"Oh, believe me, we did." Amanda leaned in and gave me a hug.

Lyle landed a quick kiss on my cheek, not caring that a muscular arm surrounded me, and I was pretty sure I heard a decisive inward sniff. Yep, Killian smelled that good and Lyle's eyes went dreamy. Killian lifted his free hand, gaining the attention of the guard at the door. "Sammy, could you see my friends out, please?"

"Sure, Killian."

Lyle and Amanda followed the guard and I was left with Killian and half his remaining teammates.

"Let me grab my bag and we'll get out of here." He dropped his arm from my shoulder and grabbed my hand. We passed a comfortable sitting area and kept going into the main part of the locker room. The huge alcoves held gear and personal items. Killian grabbed his bag and we both turned.

Stump stood in our path.

Killian's fingers tightened on mine. "Back off, Stump."

The behemoth looked at me then at Killian. "I owe your lady an apology." He turned back to me. "I'm really sorry for making a complete ass of myself and doing and saying what I did."

I squeezed Killian's hand in return, and knew my face was beet red. "No worries," I assured him. "I'm going to use the experience for my college thesis."

Stump's jaw dropped and his face went red.

"I'm teasing," I said with a genuine smile.

He grinned, and from the corner of my eye, I saw Killian's lips tilt up, though his eyes still burned holes in the poor guy. "Goodbye, Stump." He used the same commanding voice he used with me.

"Goodbye, Killian. Goodbye..."

"Rebecca."

"Goodbye, Rebecca," Stump mumbled and then made a hasty retreat.

"Thank you." Killian turned his now-softened, gorgeous eyes on me.

"What for?" I asked.

"He's a nice guy when he isn't drinking. Has my back when I'm on the field. He's a pain in my ass, but still a friend."

"You're welcome." My head cocked back so I could look into his eyes and I was in heaven.

He turned, gave a firm tug to my hand and I followed him out. My eyes were glued to his backside, causing me to stumble over a discarded shirt lying on the floor.

"Sorry," Killian said over his shoulder and slowed down.

"Not a problem," I said, with a smile he didn't see.

Killian didn't introduce me to any of his teammates and no one stopped us. He took me to an underground garage, and I didn't melt from the outside heat, but I still dissolved into the luxurious seat of his car. I know a low moan escaped my lips, but Killian just showed his dimples and buckled me in. I wondered what he'd do if I pulled him tightly against me and sniffed, for an hour or two.

He opened his door and folded into the seat with absolute grace despite his size.

"Ah, hell," he muttered, and turned my way. He unlatched my seat belt and pulled me close looking into my eyes before his mouth came down on mine. It was the most mouthwatering kiss I'd ever had.

His hard lips molded to mine. His tongue ran over my teeth, tasted, dipped deeper and then plunged. His hands went to my ponytail, effortlessly sliding out the elastic before spreading his fingers to either side of my scalp. He sank farther into the kiss, making promises with his lips.

He tasted so damn good.

When he pulled back, I actually moaned. The sound he made was more like the rumbling growl of a lion. He took my lower lip between his teeth and pulled slightly before letting go. He put distance between us and I immediately missed his mouth.

"We'll eat at my house." He kissed my forehead, reached over, grabbed the seat belt, and fastened me in again. My hands went to my hair as I looked around for the hair tie.

"Leave it."

I stopped my search but couldn't help running my fingers through the mussed tangles. Killian's hand captured mine. "No." A second later he added. "Please," and released my fingers.

Okay, I was a pushover and didn't have much experience with guys, but I had some. I should have argued, straightened my hair anyway, or even voiced some sort of displeasure. But the *please* did it. An intense electrical pulse shot straight between my thighs.

I left my hair alone and he didn't speak the remainder of the drive.

CHAPTER SIX

KILLIAN CLICKED A BUILT-IN switch above our heads and the wrought iron gates opened into a different world. He hadn't touched or looked at me since our vocabulary demise. It was disconcerting, but I thought he might have some idea of how sexually attracted I was to him.

He drove up the long driveway, clicked another control, and went straight into the monstrous garage. I had just enough time to notice a huge truck and little else.

"Don't touch that door," he ordered.

My hand had automatically lifted to the handle. There was something to be said for his manners when it came to gentlemanly behavior, but he negated it with commands.

He opened my door, grasped my hand and walked me into his home. Again, I had little time to appreciate the finer details because he pulled me past the kitchen, an entertainment room, took me around a corner, down a long hallway, and into his bedroom. It was a huge house, but I had no doubt this was his room because an incredible scent permeated the air. His scent.

My eyes immediately went to one of the largest beds I'd ever seen. Slowly, I turned back to Killian. He released my hand and peered deeply into my eyes without saying a word.

I began to grow self-conscious, but then his hand came out and his fingers grazed the side of my hair. At the same time, his thumb skimmed across my cheek, sending shivers clear to my toes. I watched him exhale a long breath and ever so slowly he moved closer. His other hand came up and his lips seared mine. It was like the first kiss, but more earth shattering. He slowly explored my mouth, causing my pulse to accelerate. His tongue dipped and teased, discovered and demanded. No one had ever kissed me like this.

The rest of my body screamed for attention as the kiss continued. I sighed into his mouth, but he wouldn't take the hint and just kept his fingers in my hair and one palm on my jaw. My hands came up to his biceps and I gave a small squeeze that he probably didn't feel. The strength in his arms turned my sigh into a moan, causing him to release my lips and move an inch back.

"We should talk," his silken voice purred.

Maybe for once in my life honesty would pay off. "I don't want to talk."

I saw his dimples flash and before I knew what happened he pulled the hem of my t-shirt over my head. He took a moment to gaze at my tank-top tan line and my pink bra. His dimples grew more pronounced. His hands came up and his thumbs slid down inside the bra cups, grazing my nipples. He jerked the material to the side and down, startling me as my breasts came free.

"Heaven," he breathed against my naked flesh as his head bent and he took one nipple into his mouth.

I went to my tiptoes, awash in pleasure, and wasn't sure if my legs would hold me. Like he'd done to my mouth, he leisurely worshipped my breasts. I sank my hands into his sable hair, so soft and divinely perfect. He turned us slightly without taking his mouth away from my breast. I followed his lead, walking backward until I felt the mattress against the back of my legs. My breast slipped from his lips as he nudged me to sit.

He released me and stood, pulling his shirt over his head. It landed on the floor.

He simply stared at my naked breasts and his heavy breathing filled the room. I stared too. Killian MacGregor's chest was rippled muscle and the definition of mouth-watering perfection. I wanted to lick every valley.

"Take the bra off," he said so huskily, I shivered.

With a mind of their own, my hands traveled behind me to unhook my bra. But then, modesty reared its head because my breasts were misshaped by the pulled-back cups. Placing my hands behind me would only accent how ridiculous I thought they looked.

A low rumble came from his throat and his dimples disappeared. "You think too much. Take it off."

There was no please, but he was right. I did think too much.

He stood waiting as I fought my insecurities.

My hands went behind me again and his eyelids lowered slightly as his gaze continued to admire my chest. I unclipped the back and pulled my arms forward, relieving the awkward pressure from the cups and took off my bra.

His eyes sizzled. "Beautiful."

For the first time in my life, I didn't feel inadequate. Killian left no doubt that he believed what he said, but more than that, I believed him.

"Lie back for me." He only touched me with his thick voice, and the words sizzled though my veins.

I sank back into the softest comforter in the world. I took a quick intake of air when he grasped my foot. My shoe went flying behind him. A long caress slithered over my calf before he released my foot and lifted my right ankle. His touch left a scorching trail along my leg, sending molten energy straight between my thighs. He slowly lowered my leg, bringing his hands to the fastening of my capris. His fingers slid down my legs, hooking my panties in the same movement. I was bare in no time.

His voice dripped with red-hot need. "Fuck, I want to look at you for hours, but I'm done being nice. You ready, Legs?"

Speech was completely beyond me, but I managed to smile, which he took as a yes because his pants and boxer briefs dropped to the floor. I had only a few seconds to admire his full erection before his body covered mine.

"Wrap your legs around my hips."

I was past caring that he demanded everything and was ready to follow any direction he gave. My legs circled him and he picked up my body. On his knees, he scooted me back a few feet on the bed. He made it seem effortless.

All thought left my muddled brain when he said, "Drop your legs."

My feet went to the mattress and his fingers went to the place between my thighs that needed his touch like I needed air to breathe. He explored the slick, swollen contours, as his body slid down mine. I couldn't help my gasp for breath when his mouth found me. My heels dug in and my ass lifted off the bed. His firm hand slid to my abs and pushed my hips back down onto the comforter. His eyes. Oh god his eyes. He gazed directly into mine with what felt like fire. So damn hot.

I had no idea where it came from but embarrassment creeped into my brain. The back of my head hit the pillow at the same time I tightly closed my eyes.

"On your elbows. Watch me."

His hot breath fluttered across me, sending shivers over my sensitized flesh. Ever so lightly his teeth pulled on my clit and I practically flew to my forearms.

"You're thinking again, Legs. Just feel. And watch." His voice did as much damage to my control as his lips were doing.

He sucked the sensitive nerves past his teeth while his hand remained on my stomach, adding slight pressure to keep my lower half against the bed. While breathing erratically, I watched and slid the tip of his tongue through the same folds his fingers discovered.

I was incredibly close to the fastest orgasm of my life when his hand left my stomach and two fingers slid inside me. There was no resistance and I welcomed the entry. I couldn't help myself and my arms slid down as my head fell back and a moan escaped my lips. My legs quivered while pulsing heat encompassed every nerve ending contained between my thighs, centering in my clit. Writhing spasms left me gasping for breath, while the most exquisite orgasm of my life poured through me.

Killian moved up my body before the orgasm ended and his lips met mine; warm and insistent. He drank in the endless involuntary sounds I made as the vibrations continued. He pulled away and I vaguely registered the crinkle of a condom wrapper.

Moments later, my muscles clenched around the slow, thick glide of his cock. He filled me completely before sliding nearly out. My whimper of protest earned me a deep, sexy command.

"Legs around my hips," he ground out.

I wrapped them around his backside, tilting my pelvis up. With his hands on my hips, he drove in deep and the world exploded even more insistently.

Oh, my fuck.

CHAPTER SEVEN

T HE COVERS WERE NOW pushed to the bottom of the bed. Killian held me curled with my back against his chest, my legs pulled slightly into my stomach. He'd arranged me how he wanted me then skimmed his fingers from my hip past my knee. God this man's touch drove me wild even in my sexually exhausted state.

"You hungry?" he asked minus the husky growl from earlier.

The words broke the spell, but it took me a moment to switch from my prefrontal cortex orgasmic part of my brain to the lateral hypothalamus hunger part. He waited patiently, never stopping the lazy slide of his fingers.

"Starving."

He rose from the bed, totally unconcerned with his nakedness. I looked at the hand he held out. My nudity caused me to hesitate.

"Um." I sat up, ignoring his hand, and made a grab for the rumpled sheet.

His fingers closed around mine. "Naked, in my kitchen, now."

"No way," I yelped.

I wasn't sure what to expect with my rebellion, but even so, I was surprised over what I got.

His dimples flashed and be began laughing. "You're something else; you know that Legs?"

Should I be insulted or not?

He walked over and picked up my panties, then snagged his underwear from his pants. He tossed mine on the bed while gracefully stepping into his.

I pointedly looked at the other clothes on the floor.

"This is the only concession you're getting." He had that steel tone back in his voice.

Before I knew what he was doing, he snatched up my panties and grabbed my foot. We fought over my underwear for two seconds before his hands pressed both of mine to the bed.

"Too late. Hold still." The gruff words held a challenge, and all the fight went out of me.

"Come on," he said as soon as he had my underwear in place.

My heart thumped painfully against my chest and that delicious ache between my thighs began all over again. He latched his hand to mine and pulled me reluctantly behind him.

This was not happening.

He stopped in the center of his kitchen and turned. His head dipped and he devoured every inch of me with his eyes. I stood still, fighting the need to cross my hands over my breasts.

"You are the fucking hottest woman I've ever seen." His voice came out in a low, throaty growl. "I watched you at that fucking party and couldn't take my eyes away. I wanted to beat the holy hell out of Stump, take you to the closest room, wrap those endless legs around my hips, and fuck you until you screamed."

My hands remained at my sides and my legs turned to jelly.

"You're not a screamer, though." His dimples flashed and heat raced to my cheeks. "Maybe I can change that."

Damn. I seriously didn't know if my legs could hold me up any longer. He turned and grabbed a hand towel from a drawer beside him.

"Here."

I stared down at the black towel then looked back up in question.

"If you need something to throw at me. And do not," his eyes went to my breasts, "cover those tits."

I stood frozen.

He pulled me in close, his hands going to my ass as he whispered against my ear, "Look, baby, I've eaten that pussy and sucked those delicious nipples. I know them intimately. Don't feel embarrassed or ashamed. I've dreamed of you naked in my house." He breathed a few times. "I'm controlling. I know that and I've conceded more than I want. Fucking work with me, okay?"

The words held a slight edge, but his eyes looked desperate. I took a breath, backed away, and walked to the barstool. I hitched my foot onto the top rung of the barstool, and lifted my body slightly so I could sit. His eyes followed each movement and I felt an incredible sense of power slide through me.

Yes, I felt a touch of modesty, too, but I also watched almost every inch of Killian's unadorned, ripped body move around the kitchen. He was gorgeous, and while he prepared our meal, he flicked his eyes my way countless times and made me feel the same.

I fought laughing over the fact that I was sitting in Killian MacGregor's kitchen, nearly naked, after the best sex of my life. I gave him a shy grin, but a small part of my modesty floated away.

He slid the large freezer door open and made it look sexy. The entire refrigerator in my small apartment would fit inside. He removed a casserole dish and frozen steaks that appeared cooked.

"Marty, my chef, does my shopping and comes in once a week to prepare meals. He cooked these on the grill so I can heat everything in the oven. We'll have a salad first while they warm."

He arranged the glass dish and steaks in the oven then began removing more items from the fridge.

"Do you want help?" I was impressed that my voice sounded normal.

"No, I've got this. A salad I can handle. Warming food I can handle. If there ever comes a time that someone needs me to cook from scratch, I'll beg for that offered help."

My smile widened. "You can't cook."

His dimples flashed. "If it comes from a can, I'm a gourmet chef." I laughed along with him. Then his face grew serious. "When you meet Marty, please don't piss him off. I need the calories because I burn them off too quickly. There are too many preservatives and junk in takeout. He keeps me healthy and fueled. He non-replaceable."

Killian thought I would be around to meet his once-a-week cook. Could a smile actually split someone's face?

He placed large glasses of water on the counter, followed by our salads before sitting with me. His black boxer briefs covered enough of him that I guessed he was comfortable. My panties were skimpy and the leather stuck to my ass cheeks. I stood and placed the towel on the seat so I had a layer of soft cloth covering the stool.

Killian winked at me.

I turned my eyes to the food and stabbed assorted lettuce and vegetables with my fork before lifting it to my lips. His gaze followed the movement, so I stopped before opening my mouth, wondering silently about what grabbed his attention.

"It's hard not to fuck again right now." His eyes smoldered, and my entire body grew hot.

"Wearing clothes would have helped with that," I said flippantly.

His eyes actually went darker and traveled over every inch of my exposed skin. "You really think so?" he asked after his eyes came back to mine.

I ate without tasting anything.

"Where do you run?" he asked after my first few bites.

"Uhm, around campus." Please don't let me return to broken-up speech patterns, I thought to myself.

He grinned. "Define campus. How far do you run?"

This was a safe subject, so I managed to control my stuttering for once and answered in probably the longest sentence I'd spoken thus far.

"About fifteen miles a day. I begin at my apartment and have a measured route so I can keep track of my time and distance. Twice a week I run with the team. That schedule will pick up after the first of the year, but for now, it's my off-season routine."

"Spend the night."

I blinked several times at his quick change in subject.

He gave me a lopsided grin. "Things are about to get fuck-all hectic in my life. I don't handle relationships well during football season. I'd like you to stay the night."

My heart dropped. I wouldn't be meeting his cook. I looked away, feeling tears well behind my eyes like some stupid heartsick teenager.

"Hey," his fingers hooked my chin and turned my head his way. "It doesn't mean I won't try. I need to stay focused during the season and most women can't handle it."

"Focused?"

"Football is what I eat, live, and breathe. I make no excuses and I get paid a hell of a lot of money to be the best. I'm a poor loser and not even my mother wants to be around when that happens. I want to give you tonight and tomorrow before you judge me on more than what you'll see when the regular season starts."

Really, when I thought about it, none of this made sense. "Why me?"

"Truth." He stared intently into my eyes. "The party. I watched you look away from anyone involved in more than light sexual contact. I watched you try to make that long, gorgeous body compact and unseen. You wanted nothing to do with that world, but there was something that drew me into those beautiful blue eyes."

"I didn't know you were watching," I whispered.

He gave me a long, measured look before his voice lowered another notch. "And that could be the biggest reason you're sitting nearly naked in my kitchen right now."

His eyes captured me in their endless dark depths, but the stupid words tumbled out anyway. "I could be frigid."

His laughter burst throughout the room. Like everything else he did, it was full and uninhibited, dimples fully displayed. Shivers slid straight to my sensitive lady parts.

Yes, I could make babies with this man.

The oven timer went off and, still laughing, he got up and removed the meal. I noticed the growing outline of his cock beneath the cotton of his underwear before bringing my eyes up and meeting his knowing smile.

I could smell the food now and my stomach growled. I ate salads as a warmup, Like Killian, I needed real calories for the number of miles I ran.

He prepared our plates and carried them over. The first bite put me in heaven and I started eating in earnest. I would not be upsetting Marty. Even warmed in an oven, the food was divine.

At one point, I noticed Killian staring.

I gave him a sheepish look. "Sorry, I like food."

He looked at my breasts then back up to my face. "I like you."

If I still had food in my mouth I would have choked. He started eating again while I tried to pretend his words didn't affect me as much as they did. The man should come with a warning label.

Something else bothered me, so I asked. "Why did this," I pointed to my naked chest then to his, "take so long?"

He knew exactly what I was asking.

"I didn't want an uncomplicated fuck and I had to take care of a few things first."

Did that make me a complicated fuck? "Things?"

"Yes."

I didn't feel so good about "things," but decided to like the idea of being complicated. From his one-word answer, he made it obvious I wasn't getting more from him.

I helped with the dishes, but he only allowed me in the kitchen so he could torture me. A whisper of touch against my breasts or a light kiss. His body brushed mine and he made the dishes sexual torture. His teasing made me forget the smidgen of shame I had over my nudity.

As soon as we finished, he lifted me up to the kitchen counter. The hard fullness, hidden by his underwear, pressed against me and I now craved skin on skin. The tingling along my inner thighs made me ready for more.

He played with a small piece of hair on my shoulder while kissing and nipping my neck and collarbone. I squeezed him with my thighs, hoping he'd press closer. He dropped my hair and skimmed his fingers down my sides, trailing across my legs with leisurely strokes. I shivered with need, but he never touched me where I wanted it most.

A low rumbling sound escaped my throat and he stopped and moved slightly away so he could see my face.

His voice was deep, sexy, and oh so smart-ass. "You never answered my question. Will you stay the night?"

I understood the game now and couldn't help my frustrated response. "Blackmail?"

He leaned in so his nose touched mine. "Whatever it takes."

I released an irritated sigh knowing I didn't want to win this game. "Yes, I'll stay the night. If I must," I tacked on just to be flippant.

He laughed, totally disabusing me of any power I thought I had, while swinging me into a cradle against his chest. I put my arms around his neck as he carried me back to bed.

Two incredible rounds of earth-shattering sex later, he ran a bath in his extra-large bathtub. His muscular legs rested on either side of me, and my head tiredly leaned back against his chest. His fingers ran up my arms, over my breasts, and down to my hips.

Killian MacGregor was a toucher, and I wanted his fingers doing exactly what they were doing for the rest of my life. When it came to him, I couldn't help being a fool. I'd had exactly two lovers slash boyfriends in my life, fallen in love with both, and cried my eyes out when they left me. Greg was the worst because he was my first sexual encounter and I wanted him desperately; wanted his ring, his babies, and a happily ever after. Steve didn't hurt quite so much because I expected it. Losing Killian would be devastating and I already knew it would happen. My habit of dreaming future babies was a problem and I didn't know how to stop it.

"Whatcha thinking about?"

In this, I couldn't be honest. Men did not want to hear that you were thinking about the pounds of chocolate you'd eat when they dumped you. And most of all they didn't want to know you were thinking about the little baby bot you would have that looked just like his father. I was a throwback to the fifties and I'd been this way since I fell in love with a boyband member.

"My clothes, running shoes, clean underwear, you know, girly things that make our lives livable."

His chest muscles rippled under my cheek as he laughed.

"I need to be at the stadium at six tomorrow morning for film. I'll give you a ride home after that. You can change into running clothes and then I'll run with you."

He couldn't see my grin. "Okay."

He tipped my chin up so I looked into his eyes. "The rest of tomorrow is mine."

I loved the sound of that. "Do we have plans?"

His fingers slipped over my leg and delved high between my thighs.

"It depends on how this feels."

"Mmm, it feels really good," I said, not realizing what he meant.

"Then I didn't pound it hard enough." His entire palm staked its claim as he cupped me.

"Oh." I had permanent hot-flash, red-face syndrome around him.

His chest rumbled again.

My mouth opened and the words spilled out before I could stop myself, "Do men get chaffed?"

I could hear his laughter now as he answered, "Not from this," he slid a finger inside me. "At least it's never happened to me, but there's a first time for everything."

"You're teasing me."

"You're fun to tease."

We fell asleep in his bed after I tried my damnedest to chafe his cock.

Chapter Eight

KILLIAN'S ALARM WENT OFF. He kissed my forehead and rolled out of bed in complete darkness. He explained the night before that watching film of the coming week's rival team was the easiest part of his week.

I grumbled and fell back to sleep and dreamed about that baby boy with Killian's dimples. My eyes popped open when the covers were yanked away. I squinted against the light shining through the open blinds.

He held a tray in his arms. "One of the few things I can cook, sleepyhead, is waffles, and I make a mean cup of coffee."

"No coffee. Not till after I run." My voice was still groggy with sleep.

"Sit up. I'll drink yours, and you can have my water."

I adjusted the pillows behind my back, looked at the pushed down covers, and glanced at him while trying to snag the sheet.

He shook his head and gave me his "just-try-it" look.

Killian was really into this naked thing, though he was completely dressed. All my insecurities resurfaced.

"You shouldn't drink coffee before running," I said grumpily to hide my awkwardness. I had heard that it was actually good for you, but I needed something to say.

He scanned my bare breasts. "In the morning, there's no blood in my veins, just coffee. Now stop complaining and enjoy your breakfast."

"One waffle. I can't eat a lot before I run."

"I'm taking notes. Are all runners this picky?"

"What do you eat before a game?"

"A cow."

I glared. "Seriously."

"Okay, so I eat light, but the cow comes later."

"Exactly," I said in a harsher tone than I meant to.

"You sure are grouchy in the morning."

The gruff voice he used to make me sizzle was back and damn, his dimples were showing. As hard as I tried to keep a level tone, my words came out breathy. "Only when I've had less than five hours sleep."

Killian wasn't fooled. "I'll add that to the list."

I ate one waffle, wanted five more, but knew I needed to run first. Killian gave me a clean pair of his boxer briefs, sweat shorts, and a t-shirt. I showered quickly while he took care of pressing emails. I walked into the front room looking like a homeless person in the oversized clothes.

His dimples flashed and I wanted to drown in his laughing eyes.

Rounding my shoulders, I tilted my upper body back and displayed a double peace sign with my fingers before tilting forward again. "I got this gangsta shit down," I said.

Killian was on me in a blink, spinning me around, my ass in the air with my stomach pressed against the back of the couch. He had my shorts and underwear pushed to the floor before I knew what happened.

"Killian, what are you doing?" I laughed.

"You in my territory, and you payin' turf fee."

I could only groan as his cock slid between inside me and found that sweet spot. He fingered my clit while his hips went to work rocking the large couch. God, I could get used to this every day for the rest of my life.

I moaned when the orgasm zinged inside me. Killian roared against the skin of my neck. I might not be a screamer, but he sure as hell made up for it. I liked it because he always let me know I'd done something right. Even if all I did was have repeated orgasms.

Sliding out, he pulled up my underwear and shorts then turned me around.

For the first time after sex, he didn't look happy.

"Fuck, I'm sorry," he said with complete shock on his face.

What the hell?

His eyes locked with mine and I saw worry tinged with something I couldn't identify. On anyone else I would think it was terror.

"I didn't bag it."

Oh shit, it was terror.

"Um, I'm on the pill."

He still didn't look happy.

"I'm clean and haven't had sex in over a year." I said.

His dimples gave a slight quirk. "I'm clean, too. Why are you on the pill?"

My face went red. I did not feel comfortable talking about my body's cycle.

He waited patiently.

I gave in. "Running makes my period almost non-existent. I take the pill straight through for three months then off for a week. It sometimes lets my body do its thing."

He blinked, and then a slow, sensual smile lit up his face.

"You don't have periods for three months?" He looked like he ate a piece of his favorite candy.

"Perv."

"Why have I never dated a runner before?"

Now I gave him my evil-eyed look.

"Sorry." He turned slightly away. "I'm an insensitive jerk. What about mood swings?"

My fist flew, hitting him on the side of his arm. I shook my hand out from the pain of connecting with cement.

"What was that for?" He rubbed the spot I'd hit even though I knew it really felt like nothing more than a mosquito bite to him.

"That was a mood swing."

He laughed all the way to the counter where he grabbed his keys.

He turned back with his bad-boy grin still plastered on his face. "I'll add that to my long list of notes."

An hour later, we stood outside my apartment building after I changed into real running gear. As much as I liked wearing Killian's clothes, I couldn't run in them. He had a ball cap pulled low over his eyes, no shirt, and drool-worthy shorts. Unfortunately, I couldn't afford to grow breathless, so I kept my eyes off him or at least tried. It was nine in the morning, four hours after I usually started my run, and it was already hotter than hell.

"You sure you want to do this?" I asked Mac the Knife.

"I'm tough, baby. I live for this heat."

He held tight on the first mile, stretched with me, and then without complaint settled in for the real fun. Five miles later, I started to see the strain. Sweat dripped off both our bodies, but his was a river.

"Cut the coffee next time," I taunted. We continued running for two more miles.

We ran beside the canal and entered the soccer park district. He grabbed my hand, throwing me slightly off stride.

"What are you doing?"

He pulled me off the cement and onto the grass. Three small trees bunched close together and had about five feet of shade beneath them. He collapsed and pulled me down beside him.

"We have another six miles." I struggled to pull away, but he wouldn't release my hand.

"I think we need an ambulance, and you can't leave me to face the tabloids alone." His heavy breathing made me smile.

"Tabloids?"

"'Killian MacGregor Dead From Heatstroke' will be the headline. If you mention coffee, I'm throwing you into the canal."

I couldn't help the giggle that escaped. "You did better than I thought you would."

"Hell, what does it take to be at the head of the pack for college runners? I can run, baby, but not at this level."

"You have too much muscle mass. Your body works harder." I looked at the canal and tried to keep more laughter from my voice. "The coffee and five waffles didn't help."

"I'm too tired to take notes, so please remind me after the ambulance arrives."

I flipped open my old cheap phone and called Lyle. "Killian went running with me. We're at the canal soccer field." I listened and then answered. "He doesn't have a shirt on and his shorts will give you wet dreams for the next month."

I looked at Killian, who put his forearm over his eyes. I clicked my phone shut.

He groaned out beneath his arm, "Can I just look sexy and not put out?"

My laughter bubbled over. I think I loved Killian Mac-Gregor.

CHAPTER NINE

LYLE MADE THE TRIP worth his time. He ogled and leered, lifting his eyebrows and making a complete cake of himself. That was Lyle, and surprisingly Killian didn't seem to mind and even played along.

"Thanks for saving me. I think I'm giving up jogging. I'll just stick to weights."

"Excellent idea. Weights are good." Ogle, leer, eyebrow lift.

This went on even after Killian took us to a late breakfast. I scarfed, both men watched, and I didn't care.

"Does she eat like this all the time?" Killian questioned Lyle.

"I've invested in pizza stock and made a fortune. She puts away a large, topped with everything, and wants to know what's for dessert afterward. Touch a pizza slice or her dessert and lose a finger. Not with a knife or anything, she'll just bite it off and eat it."

"Ha ha, funny," I said.

Amanda and Lyle always teased me about food. Killian was great to go out with because he actually managed to eat a little more than I did. If I added the five waffles he ate earlier, he was holding his own.

Lyle dropped us off at my apartment. Killian followed me inside and, as soon as the door closed, pulled me into his body. I could feel every hard, hot, and needy inch of him.

"What's your schedule like tomorrow?"

I pulled away slightly, giving him a quizzical look.

"Tomorrow?" he repeated.

"Uh, I have a nine o'clock class."

"Pack an overnight bag and I'll get you there on time."

I took a slow breath to line up my thoughts. "Don't you have practice or something?"

"Yes, practice and something, but I'm not finished with you."

"Finished?" That feeling of dread entered my stomach again.

He ignored the look I knew was on my face. "What's your weekly schedule look like?"

I was missing something here but went ahead and acted like an idiot. "Weekly schedule?"

He smiled slow and easy, moved back slightly, giving me room, and smiled some more.

I stared.

"I thought maybe you could concentrate more if my dick wasn't touching you."

My eyes dropped to the front of his shorts which were tented. No smart comeback came to mind. I just licked my lips.

His voice dipped to that sweet, sexy octave that made me salivate.

He laughed but stayed back. "I want to know your schedule so maybe sometime during the week we can connect. Mine is crazy right now, but once regular season begins, things will be worse."

I barely managed to keep my eyes up and not look at his crotch again. "I have classes on Monday, Tuesday, and Friday. I have Wednesday days off but work all night."

"Work where?"

"Tillomans."

His eyebrows arched. "I've never seen you there."

"I've been there for five months, just on Wednesday evenings." Tillomans was an exclusive restaurant that had steep prices, world-class dining, and excellent tips. It's challenging to get a job there but the college arranged it for me.

"Friday nights?" He looked hopeful.

"Open."

"Saturday and Sunday nights?"

"Open."

"Not anymore. Pack essentials, maybe a couple nice dresses for dining out. You can buy anything you need that you don't bring. When we're alone at the house, you won't need clothes." He moved closer so he was back in my personal space and threaded his fingers into my hair, holding my face still. "I want you on the weekends when I'm in town. Half the season I'm away, but when I'm not, I want you with me. Bring that sexy short skirt, too."

Dimples.

I had trouble breathing.

My life had gone from zero to Killian MacGregor in twenty-four hours. I was in love.

He stayed close while I packed a medium-sized bag. I was having trouble believing this man, face of an angel, body of a god, rich, sports icon, and light years beyond sexy wanted me. I packed a bag for sleepovers and everything that went with it.

And just like that, all my insecurities came rushing to the surface. I managed to hide them as I stuffed my things inside the bag. I tossed in my extra running shoes, received a scowl, which only made me smile, and zipped my bag. Killian took the handle, though it had rollers, and followed me to the door. I locked it and walked slightly behind him, watching his ass all the way to his car. His arm muscles barely tightened while holding my bag, damn it. I should have packed more junk.

We pulled up in front of a large outdoor mall. Killian got out first, came around, and assisted me from the car. I glanced at the storefronts, seeing no reason for us to be there. He took my hand and walked me toward a high-end cosmetic retail salon. I had no clue about his intentions.

"Pick out your soap, shampoo, and makeup, whatever you want so you don't need to bring it back and forth from my place to your apartment."

He walked inside. I followed in stunned silence.

All female heads turned. Killian stayed by my side as I tentatively picked out the things I needed.

I looked at him. "Are you buying anything?"

His gaze tilted down to mine and he smiled. "No."

When I went to dig into my small purse, he pulled out some bills from his wallet and paid for everything. When we were back in his car and pulling onto the main road, I couldn't help myself. "I can pay for my own things, Killian."

He actually looked surprised for a split second and turned my way quickly giving me his completely lovable grin.

"I'll add that to the list."

He knew exactly how to take the angst out of me. I decided to change the subject. "So, what's your weekly schedule?"

He didn't hesitate. "Strength training in the mornings, full pads and contact most afternoons. My masseuse comes to the house at six thirty Monday through Friday evenings, and I have a standing sports psychologist session on Wednesday nights."

I wasn't going to comment on the psychologist, but he answered my questions for me right after he took my hand and ran his fingers over my knuckles.

"I have a temper and don't handle losing well. There are other things I don't handle with full brain function either. He quickly glanced at me then back to the road. I've never hit a woman, never will. As you saw with Stump. My trigger is hair thin. When I got the starting QB position, it was suggested that I see a sports shrink."

Wow. Okay, I knew lots of athletes used hypnotists and therapists, but he was the first one I knew who went to one for anger issues. I looked up from our locked fingers.

"Do you think I could borrow him when track season starts?"

His dimples came back.

Chapter Ten

After we arrived at Killian's house, he took me out back to his humungous swimming pool. I hadn't packed my suit and looked around for a way out.

"You won't need it," he said with a sexy leer, obviously guessing what caused my anxiety.

He stripped me down, then himself, and pulled my hand until the water surrounded us. It was perfect. He began swimming laps while I leaned back on a rounded step covered by a large blue awning to give me shade and watched.

Maybe he was a nudist. I'd never known anyone so comfortable in their naked skin. I admired his arms as he ate up the length of the pool, turned around, and repeated the process. I lost count of his laps and just enjoyed the pool's cool water and my favorite pair of arms in the entire world. His naked ass propelling through the water wasn't bad either.

Eventually, those big powerful arms brought him to me. He circled my hips and lifted me half out of the pool. My palms rested on his shoulders as he held me up. For the first time, outside of me being above him in bed, I looked down at Killian MacGregor.

He was undeniably glorious.

Water dripped from his long eyelashes and streams trailed down his face and chest. His eyes stayed on mine as he lowered me, ever so slowly, with just the strength in his arms. I was Tinker Bell again. He stood me on the second step with his feet at pool level.

"Mmm. I like this," he said in that husky, sexy voice of his.

His mouth, now even with my breast, sucked me in. Not just the nipple, but as much of my breast as he could. No man had ever done that, and the feeling was incredibly erotic. My head went back and a low moan escaped from my throat. He switched sides and I moaned again. His mouth released my breast and I looked down. He stared at me as his tongue twirled around my nipple. He played, sucked, teased, and watched me the entire time.

I wondered somewhere in the back of my brain, if a girl could have an orgasm with breast stimulation only. Killian pulled me a little closer so my chin rested on the top of his head. I circled my legs around his hips. He sucked my full breast in again and a cry left my throat as ripples of ecstasy ran throughout my entire body.

He held me close until my body returned to normal, or as normal as it could with my legs wrapped around Killian's bare hips.

"Better," he said against my skin after tilting me back and lowering his head.

"Better?" I asked, still woozy from the orgasm.

"I like hearing you make noise." He kissed my abs, flicking his tongue over my flesh and making me shiver all over again.

I felt embarrassed over his comment about me making noise.

"Truth. What are you thinking?"

I shifted back and his intense eyes stared into mine.

Honesty apparently mattered with him. "That you make me feel uncomfortable when you say things like that."

"Good."

I wouldn't do it. I would not do it. "Good?" Damn it.

"You need to let go and stop thinking so much when I'm fucking you."

He pulled me off the step against his chest and kissed me. Each time his lips met mine it was better than the last. He worked my mouth like he worked my body.

In fifth grade, I was five foot nine inches tall. Taller than every teacher I'd ever had. I was awkward, gangly, and homely as hell. The girls didn't play with me, the boys ran in the opposite direction. I turned inward.

It wasn't until high school that I started running. Slowly my coordination improved along with a small bit of confidence. Not in my looks or my size, but in my ability to be alone and enjoy things I could do by myself.

Being a track star got me no high school points in the hallways, but it gained attention from the newspapers and college scouts. I accepted the full ride to State and found a new world where acceptance wasn't required.

Academia was my best friend until I met Amanda and Lyle. Most people would think we had nothing in common. Amanda was studying to be a kindergarten teacher and Lyle a stage actor/director. But each of us, in our own way, was a square peg in a round hole. We didn't fit until you put our pieces against each other and then we locked tight.

Now I was naked in a swimming pool with Killian Mac-Gregor and he made me feel beautiful. And hell. I wanted nothing more than to completely let go and scream.

Killian continued pressing his body against mine and his need was far past obvious. I let my fingers do the walking down his side and over his hip until I could wrap them tightly around his cock. I wanted to taste him so badly. Killian hadn't given me any indication that he wanted my lips on him. I loved his lips on me, so turn-around was only fair.

I pulled slightly away and gathered every ounce of courage I could find.

"I want to taste you."

He closed his eyes for a moment. "Not here. Come."

He took my hand and I followed. He dried us both off with one towel before we entered his house. He stopped at his couch, tossed a pillow on the floor, and turned toward me. I arranged the pillow and sank to my knees while he stood.

I looked up past his glorious cock, over his abs and chest and then met his eyes. "I'm not sure I'm very good at this."

His lips quirked and his low, husky voice showed his need. "Christ, just taste, baby."

So, I did. Our bodies were so different, but I loved the way he used his lips and fingers on me, so I did the same. I explored with my mouth, and, at one point, palmed the sack of his balls. I wasn't sure how much pressure the silky full skin could take, so I squeezed just a little. He took my hand and squeezed mine harder, teaching me what he liked. I writhed against his mouth when he did this to me and I wanted a similar reaction from him. His straining cock slid past my lips until my tongue felt the pulse along the backside, which signaled his pending orgasm. He grabbed my hair and held my head in place while pulling away. He took hold of his cock and spurted across my breasts.

I looked up. Killian focused on his cock and my breasts. It was too damn sexy. For the first time in my life, I looked down at my small breasts, covered in milky white semen, and saw something beautiful.

❦❦❦❦❦ ❦❦❦❦❦

We napped later in the afternoon, made more of Marty's delicious frozen concoctions for dinner, and watched a movie on Killian's larger-than-life television screen. I had a small blanket pulled over my completely naked body. Killian leaned back with his legs spread, wearing a pair of gray boxer briefs. My head rested on his thigh and his hand ran lazily through my hair. I loved every minute.

Killian dropped me off at my apartment at seven the next morning. I was tired, but in a good way. Now I was preparing for my class while he went to the stadium and did his professional thing. He would pick me up Friday after practice, and we would get one more weekend before he flew to Seattle the following week.

I was having trouble with the thought of not seeing him over the next five days. When he flew out of town, it would be much longer. Only one weekend in bed with the sex slash football god and my heart clenched at the thought.

In forty-eight hours, I was now zero to Killian MacGregor, in love, and totally addicted to sex.

Chapter Eleven

T HE WEEK WENT BY like a Zoom call where everyone's frozen. Killian called each night sounding tired and irritable, but he said he just wanted to hear my voice before he kicked it.

Other than his nightly voice, the week basically sucked until Thursday when I met my crew at a local restaurant bar. Amanda and Lyle were there before me and somehow managed to get a booth in the back corner away from prying ears. I knew they were both capable of camping out in the parking lot until the place opened to get that booth. I also knew they wanted the inside scoop on Killian.

They sat across the table with me in the inquisition seat. We ordered our drinks. I acted normal, took my time looking at the menu, and basically played it cool.

"What the fuck, sis?" Lyle broke first.

I glanced up. "Huh?"

Amanda jerked the menu from my hands and slammed it down on the table. I started laughing.

"You are cruel." Amanda had her best bitch voice.

"Yes, I am, but you guys don't really expect me to give details do you?"

"Yes," they practically shouted at the same time.

"He's incredibly hot." I waited a beat, seeing displeasure written on both faces. "All over." I felt heat rise in my cheeks.

"Now we're getting somewhere. Talk to a brother about size." Lyle batted his eyes.

I choked on my drink. "No." I coughed some more. "I will not."

"He's so hung," Amanda said, stretching out the "so."

"And how would you know?" I snapped back.

"Okay, so he's not hung."

"I hate you and yes, he's, god, I don't like that expression."

Amanda looked at Lyle and they both gave me evil eyes.

"You didn't show him your straitlaced side did you?" Lyle asked.

They drove me crazy, but thankfully, I loved them. "I'm staying at his place this weekend."

"He's hung." Amanda gave a knowing smile.

"Stop saying that." In exasperation, I changed the subject. "He said I could invite the two of you to the game on Sunday and he'd really like to take you out to dinner."

They didn't comment on my invitation or miss a beat.

"So, tell us about the sex. Is it good, is he kinky, did you learn anything?" Only Lyle would ask about kink.

"Compared to your kinky shenanigans, I doubt he'd compare."

"She said shenanigans," Lyle teased. "He's got to be kinky. I've had these dreams."

"No," Amanda and I said at the same time.

"Okay, but you both secretly want to know."

"Not in association with Killian," I all but groaned.

Amanda slapped Lyle on the shoulder. "You're letting her get away without telling the good stuff. You know fact is better than fantasy." She turned to me. "You owe us. Give the facts."

They were never going to leave me alone, so I took a deep breath. "He has a thing about nudity." There I said it.

"As in, he doesn't like it?" Amanda's eyes got huge.

"No, he likes it. A lot. The less clothing the better. Even in his kitchen."

Amanda shook her head. "Wait a minute. You're going along with this."

Lyle nudged her. "You're surprised?"

"With you or me, no. With Rebecca Cavanaugh, hell yes. I've only seen her completely naked once."

"Do tell." Lyle's eyebrows went up and down in his best imitation of a perv leer.

"You're gay," Amanda said with barely controlled patience.

"The two of you never seem to mind when I talk about my fuck toys. You got the inside on Miss Priss's body so I get to hear it."

"No." Now my voice was rising. "You will stop talking about my body. I'd like to enjoy dinner."

Lyle looked at Amanda. "Okay, I see your point. She couldn't possibly be living naked in Killian MacGregor's fuck pad."

I ground my teeth, but then noticed they were holding back laughter. "I hate you both."

"Na, you love us." Lyle flashed his famous smile, the one that got him some of the hottest "fuck toys" in the area. "Ropes, leather, chains?"

My forehead hit the table and I knocked it against the wood once more for added effect. I really did love them, I reminded myself. They stuck by me freshman year with Greg and then my sophomore year with Steve. My latest dry spell with no boyfriend was completely tolerable because I had them. They knew my secrets; my fantasy white-picket fence, babies, and happily ever after. They also knew as well as I did that this type of make believe rarely came true in today's modern world.

I needed to give a little here. "He bought me makeup and hair products for his house."

"Now that's kinky." Lyle rolled his eyes.

I finally gave them the PG-13 account of the weekend, telling them almost everything, just leaving out the more intimate details. I also kept the psychologist information quiet because I hadn't read anything about it online. I trusted my friends, but there were some things I didn't need to share.

I woke up Friday morning with a smile on my face. I ran twenty miles, came home, and cleaned my apartment. I got my favorite polish out and painted my toenails bright purple. Every year on my birthday, Amanda paid for me to get a mani-pedi, and then on her birthday I paid for hers. Other than that, we were on our own.

I averaged two hundred dollars in tips on Wednesday nights and used the money for utilities and food. Anything extra went into the bar jar. Before I turned twenty-one, it was the dinner jar. That money also doubled as my savings, and I now had a little over two hundred dollars. My scholarship paid my tuition and gave me a stipend toward my apartment. A small student loan each year paid the rest. I took the bus or walked, and besides my weekly party night with Amanda and Lyle, I lived cheap. Once track season started, my travel expenses, including food, were covered. I would have about ten thousand dollars in debt when I graduated, but that was a drop in the bucket compared to most students.

What I lacked in my limited budget was dress clothes. Buying off the rack at cheap clothing outlets was difficult with my height. I scoured second-hand stores and every so often came up with a winner, but I suspected they wouldn't be considered a prize in Killian's world. He said he liked my short skirt, so I decided to wear it. I had a cranberry-colored blouse that I'd never worn; I had luckily found it on clearance one time when I shopped with Amanda. Normally, I would unfasten the shirt one button below my collarbone, but I decided to brave it and leave another undone. I took a long look at myself in the mirror. With trembling fingers, I unbuttoned the blouse, removed my bra, and refastened the buttons. My body type allowed me to leave off the bra, but I'd never been brave enough. I took a deep breath and continued my preparations.

There was no question about my hair. If I put it in my favorite ponytail style, Killian would have it lose five seconds after seeing me. He had a thing for hair and he liked it messy.

When five o'clock rolled around I started pacing, too nervous to sit still.

What if he changed his mind and didn't show up? Doubt flooded in. I had come on too strong. Or maybe I wasn't up to his usual standards. Everything had happened so fast. Now he'd had time to think about it and decided I wasn't worth the trouble.

The knock startled me out of my rising panic. I opened the door, my heart pounding. He stepped into me and locked his mouth to mine. He smelled and tasted so far past good that I couldn't concentrate as my arms circled behind his neck. He placed his hands on my ass and brought my needy sex firmly against his cock. Killian was very happy to see me.

He had me anticipating sex against the front door, and I moaned when he broke the kiss. His eyes traveled down my body. On the return perusal, he undid the highest closed button on my blouse and then the next.

His dimples displayed fully with his sexy grin. "I like," he said huskily.

He twined my fingers with his and preceded me out the front door.

"Got your key?"

My hand went to my nearly naked chest.

"Leave it, baby. Do you have your key?"

"Yes, but I can't go out like this."

"I could unbutton one more and you could still go out like that. I'm starving, let's go."

He ushered me into his car before walking around and folding himself in. The engine started and we pulled away from the curb.

"Killian, please, I don't feel comfortable." Mortification caused tears to stir in my eyes.

He pulled back over to the curb, turned my way, and gave me a solemn look. "You are the sexiest woman I've ever seen. I don't understand why you hide that gorgeous body."

He leaned in and tipped my chin up. His eyes always conveyed that I was beautiful and he had a way of making me feel like a sex goddess. To tip the scales in his favor, he took my lips in a tender, do-this-for-me kiss.

What else could I do?

Chapter Twelve

Dinner with the star quarterback of the Phoenix Scorpions was not what I expected. Football fans requested autographs, asked questions about the coming season, and even took a few pictures. Killian handled it like everything else he did. He smiled, made the pictures something to remember, and talked the talk about his team.

For the most part, once our dinner arrived, they left us alone.

"Sorry about that. I should have warned you."

My teasing smile came through. "I'm sure it was hard for you the morning you took me and Lyle to breakfast and no one paid you any attention."

"The only things hard that morning were my burning calves and my cock. All I could think about was getting you home, getting you naked, and relieving my calves in the swimming pool."

I laughed then took a drink of water, looking around to see if anyone heard what he said. I was learning very quickly that teasing Killian had consequences. I'm not sure what came over me, but I decided to test the theory. I reached under the table and checked to see just how hard he was at that very moment.

A low growl came from deep in his throat. He turned slightly, reached his fingers up, and unfastened another button on my blouse. Now it was undone an inch below my breasts, though the fold of the material thankfully kept it from gaping open. I moved my trembling hand away and we went back to eating.

Mac the Knife was out of my league.

The remainder of our dinner was uneventful. It was difficult knowing people watched each move we made. Not that they cared at all about me, except maybe to wonder who I was. Killian was great at ignoring the blatant stares and asked me about my week.

I filled him in on the little things and began to relax. I couldn't help noticing his eyes drift to my semi-exposed chest and it gave me a warm fuzzy feeling inside. I liked that he liked my small breasts.

"Dessert?" he asked, pulling me from my fantasy thoughts.

I had a sweet tooth, but I hadn't seen him all week and my need for him far outweighed my need for sugar.

"No, thank you. What are our plans for the rest of the night?"

Without saying a word, Killian tossed two hundred-dollar bills on the table, took my hand. He pulled me to my feet.

His warm breath tickled across my ear. "I want to fuck you until you can't walk and then fuck you some more."

Funny how I never thought I would like blunt sexual talk, but his words caused goose bumps to run across my skin. We walked to his car with my hand tucked safely into his warm grasp. He mechanically put my seat belt on while touching me as little as possible. He caught the slight smile on my lips.

"You drive me crazy." He stood and closed the door before walking around the car.

He adjusted the station to a sports network and listened to team updates and analysis the entire drive to his house. He stopped his car closer to his front door instead of parking in the garage. My hand lifted to open the door then immediately dropped when he made a sound deep in his throat. I couldn't help smiling over his ingrained chivalry.

It was now eight thirty and the Arizona sun was finally going down. A light desert rain shower had started on our drive and the wind had picked up. Instead of Killian immediately opening my car door, I noticed through the side mirror that he lifted the trunk.

When he opened my door, he held a blanket in one hand and grabbed mine with the other. I had no idea what he was doing until he stopped on the well-manicured grass and spread out the blanket.

"It's raining."

He kneeled on the blanket facing me. His hands came around my hips and I felt the slow slide of the zipper at the back of my skirt. The material shimmied down my legs. Killian slowly pulled down my panties so they rested on my skirt. He held my hand as I stepped out of them. A light mist of water covered his face as his dark eyes traveled up my legs. He cupped my ass and buried his face in the juncture of my thighs, nuzzling his nose along my needy sex. I heard him inhale, and for all of two seconds I felt self-conscious before letting go. Killian made me feel sexy.

He leaned back and pulled his shirt over his head. It made a wet splat when it hit the grass, but my eyes were on Killian.

Trails of water ran between the grooves of rippling muscles. His heavy breathing caused his chest to rise and fall, accenting each furrow. The air was hot and heavy, even with the rain. I loved running in this weather and I was discovering that I liked wet outdoor sex, too.

Killian suddenly stood and removed his pants as fast as the drenched material allowed.

"Do you want me to take off my shirt?" The sight of him fully nude made it hard to talk.

"Hell, no," he groaned.

He lifted me and had my back pressed against the wet blanket mere seconds later. He took the bottom edges of my new shirt and tore it open. I groaned in dismay, but then his palms covered my breasts. What the hell did a cheap blouse matter?

The rain fell harder and Killian came down completely on top of me. I circled my legs around his hips as he found that secret place with his cock. He put his arms to either side of my shoulders, lifting his chest off mine while his hips slammed forward. My fingers went to his pectoral muscles, sinking my fingernails into his skin. We were drenched, with the slapping of just our bodies combined with our moans and gasps for oxygen.

Killian fucked me. It wasn't gentle or comfortable; it was more primal than I'd ever known. High, intense noises escaped my throat while Killian pushed into me harder and faster. My eyes closed against the rain and I felt every inch of him drive deeper.

I didn't fall over the edge, I plunged. My body spasmed around his cock, making me cry out. White sparks flashed behind my eyelids and his loud moan filled the night as he made one last forward thrust.

We lay there beathing heavily. My eyes slowly opened and I looked at the man above me. He held himself up using his gorgeous arms. I could just make out his facial features in the small amount of light shining from the front porch. His dimples accented his full lips.

"You're getting the hang of this, Legs," he said gruffly.

Slowly, I let my hands fall away. He lowered his chest against mine then rolled so we were side by side on the soggy blanket.

"You couldn't wait until we got inside?" My voice held embarrassed humor. Killian wanted me screaming and I'd come so close.

"I enjoy the rain."

The gruff words caused shivers to run over my skin. He pulled me tighter against him and licked water from the side of my face.

"My hair's a mess."

"Yes."

I softly slapped his arm. "You weren't supposed to agree."

He gently pulled strands of wet hair off my cheek. "I like it this way."

I decided to like it, too.

I had spent the entire week trying to figure out why Killian made me feel so good about myself. He spoke bluntly and sometimes got my feminist side up, but he always came back with something that made my breath catch. He gave brisk commands expecting to get his way and I usually gave in without argument. While we were apart, I wondered what he'd do if I didn't comply. I could tell it wasn't something he was used to. Killian MacGregor had "control freak" down to a science.

I yearned for every minute I could spend with him before it ended.

Chapter Thirteen

We dropped our clothes in the laundry room and then took a long, warm shower. Soap led to caresses and caresses to more. I was beginning to think everything with Killian led to more. We were too tired to watch a movie, so we went straight to bed after I braided my hair to ensure the wet mass wouldn't dry hairy scary. Killian patiently watched me and then as soon as we climbed into bed, he slowly removed the hair tie and unfurled my handiwork.

"Argh, you must like the Medusa look on me."

"Hmm," he said tiredly and pulled me close.

His musky, just-washed scent surrounded me as I closed my eyes and fell asleep.

The alarm woke me.

"It's Saturday," I grumbled.

"You don't run on Saturdays?"

I rolled over expecting him to be next to me, but Killian was standing beside the bed dressed in sweats. I squinted with tired eyes and noticed the brush in his hand.

"Sit up."

I tried to pull the sheet over my upper body, but he stopped me. I shouldn't have bothered, but I chalked it up to sleepiness and not thinking clearly. I sat forward and Killian ran the brush through my hair.

"You have a few interesting kinks," I said with a sigh at how good it felt.

I could hear the laughter in his voice as he continued with sure strokes, obviously trying to get my hair to lie down properly. I laughed again but wanted to kill him at the same time.

"I have interesting kinks?" he demanded in good humor.

Nearly naked when in the house, sex in the rain, no hair ties, and alarms that go off on Saturday mornings. You, sir, have kinks."

He gathered my hair behind my neck while another rumble of laughter escaped him. "Those are rules, not kinks, but I like the *sir*."

"Argh." He was joking, wasn't he?

"I'm changing one rule and letting you have a hair tie while you run."

He placed the hair tie in question around my hair.

I needed to switch gears. "I'm running?"

"Would you normally run?"

"Yes." I couldn't help the doubtful sound in my voice.

"I had my trainer map a course for you with a distance of fifteen miles. There's a paper on the kitchen counter you can take with you."

I fell in love all over again. "You're not coming with me?"

"I have a game tomorrow and don't need to be lying in a hospital bed. I'll be in the gym working man weights while you're gone."

"Man weights?"

"Yes. You don't want me all skinny and wasted away to nothing do you?" he said teasingly.

I let pretend angst enter my voice. "I'm wasted away to nothing?"

He pinched my hip, really not managing to pull any skin. "I have no idea where you put the food you consume. I've never seen a woman eat the way you do."

Okay, now I was feeling some genuine angst. "You'd prefer I ate salad."

"Fuck, no. Please eat. It drives me crazy that women don't eat, but seriously you could gain weight and still be skinny."

I had body issues and his words hurt. I looked away, but his fingers lifted my chin and turned my face so I had to meet his eyes.

"You are incredibly sexy. Every thin, tall, gorgeous inch and I wouldn't change a thing. But, woman, you can eat."

He kissed me, morning breath and all. He tasted like coffee, so I was guessing he'd been up for a while. He pulled back slightly.

"Are you running?" He slid his hand over my cheek, caressing his thumb across my jaw.

"Yes," I breathed.

"I'll meet you in the kitchen."

Damn. He walked away.

I put my running clothes on, looked in the mirror, and wet my hair to get rid of the kinks before walking to the kitchen.

The map was amazing, and my heart skipped a beat when I thought about what he'd done.

Killian followed me outside after I drank a large glass of water. He hit the button on the controller in his hand and the front gates opened.

"Hurry back." He kissed me quickly then walked inside the house.

His neighborhood was incredible. Low-hanging trees, mega-mansions, and amazing cars parked in long, gated driveways. For someone like me, I didn't even know areas like this existed in the city.

I had clicked the timer on my watch when I started. After the first mile, I did my stretches and then resumed my run. The sun was just coming over the horizon when I started, but within thirty minutes, full daylight commenced. The hot, muggy weather of late August was in full gear. I paced myself knowing my body wasn't sweating the way it would in dryer heat.

I could really get used to living in this world, but I hardened my heart and continued running until I couldn't think past each step. My lungs expanded and endorphins took over. The path was mine.

I did my final stretches under a tree in Killian's front yard before going inside. I'd planned to hit the shower, but loud rock music drew me to his workout room. He had a full gym in his home and I watched as he lowered the weights after a butterfly lift then stood to his full height. Sweat poured from his skin and his muscles bulged. He was male perfection, delicious eye candy, and for now, all mine.

He turned and I saw the same look on his face that must have been on mine. He walked over and turned off the music.

"Sit." He nodded to a bench. "Don't move."

For once I couldn't help myself. "And what if I don't want to sit?"

His eyebrows went up. "Feeling feisty after your run, I take it."

His words really weren't a question, so I didn't say anything.

He gave me a dimpled grin. "I got caught up in some email, but I'd really like to finish my workout and then get in the pool with you."

He explained why he wanted me to sit after I'd voiced an objection. Warm fuzzies centered between my thighs as I took a seat and enjoyed my view of Killian's scrumptious body.

He focused on his workout and didn't seem to know I was in the room. Killian gave absolute focus to his training and I realized, at his game when he blew the kiss, that taking his mind from the game was something special.

I so wanted his babies.

Chapter Fourteen

T HE ENTIRE DAY WAS glorious. We watched a movie after dinner and when the movie was over, we walked hand in hand to his bedroom. I'd lost count of how many times we'd had sex that day. My body ached in all the right places, and I was surprised when he settled me close and turned off the light.

"Tomorrow could be difficult for you," he said into the darkness.

His voice had that low, husky timbre that made me think of sex. "Difficult how?"

His tone turned serious but stayed low. "I have a game-day routine and it's pretty intense. I don't talk a lot and I need you to hang with it."

"I could go home in the morning and go to the game later. I really don't need to be here."

He pulled me in tighter. "I want you here."

"Okay. I'll hang." I snuggled in as close as I could, glad I wouldn't be leaving tomorrow.

With just a touch of light shining through the windows, I woke up to gentle suction on my nipple and Killian's fingers delving between my thighs.

"Is this part of your game-day routine?" My sleepy voice held a smile.

"Mmm, it is now." He raised his head and moved over me. "I'll see how I play today and decide if I'll keep this new routine. We may need to change it up to just a blow job if it taxes my strength too much."

"You're horrible," I laughed.

The slow warm glide of his cock cut off my laughter and I helped Killian start his game day.

He wasn't kidding when he said he didn't talk much. He'd warned me, but it was difficult. Hard rock music blasted from unseen speakers throughout the house. I couldn't get away from it. I finally walked into the backyard where the sound was muted, headed to the pool, sat, and swished one hand through the water. I called Amanda and put the call on speaker.

"Did you get the tickets?" I asked.

"Yep, and we're back in the skybox. Lyle and I decided to keep you as a friend even if you are dating a man far out of our league."

"No one is out of your league and you know it."

"Well, aren't you sweet? But seriously, don't forget us when you get absorbed into the flashy lifestyle of the rich and gorgeous."

My laugh wasn't very lighthearted. "You know this is short lived."

"What's that supposed to mean?" Amanda asked with a touch of pique in her voice. "Your romance just began and you're already trying to end it?"

"It's a fling. And, as my best friend, you know I never end it. The guys dump me."

"Two guys. It's only been two and neither were good enough for you. I'm reserving judgment on the football stud, but seriously, chances are he's not good enough for you either."

"Stop, please. I'm refusing to let my heart get involved here and you're not helping."

Scoffing laughter sounded from my cell phone. "That's the biggest whopper you've ever told me. You're madly in love and if you weren't, you wouldn't be having sex with him."

I heard a noise and turned. Killian stood behind me listening. He quickly backed up with a look on his face I couldn't even begin to describe.

"Sorry, Amanda, I need to go."

She heard the trepidation in my voice and stopped laughing. "You okay?"

"Yes, I'm fine. I'll see you at the game." I clicked the end button sincerely hoping I was still attending the game.

I went inside searching for Killian. The music shut off, leaving the house deathly quiet. A minute later, he walked past me from the direction of his bedroom. He grabbed his car keys from the key holder before turning my way.

"I'm taking a drive. I'll be back in time to pick you up for the game." He headed to the garage.

"Killian, I'm sorry."

He stopped, glanced over his shoulder, and pierced me with dark, intense eyes. "I can't do this right now." His voice held no emotion whatsoever.

I stood frozen and watched him leave. Never had I thought I'd be the one to hurt him. He was Killian Mac-Gregor and I was Rebecca Cavanaugh. We'd been together for a little over a week and it was too soon for the heavy feeling surrounding my heart.

Tears welled behind my eyes. If I really thought about it, Amanda was right. I wouldn't have slept with Killian unless my heart was involved. Maybe if it ended now, I could avoid the months of devastation I'd felt after Greg dumped me.

My mind stayed on Greg for a moment. He was barely a memory, and I couldn't picture his smile. I would never forget Killian's. Protecting my heart was useless. The only consolation was that if Killian was upset, it had to mean his heart was involved, too.

We'd had mind-blowing sex, talked for hours, and gotten to know each other. What we hadn't done is talk about our hopes or dreams. I thought it was too early for that kind of deep discussion, but Killian needed to know about the other two men before him. I'd planned babies with them, too. They consumed me, and I knew I was borderline co-dependent. Yes, I could stand on my own feet, support myself, and make my own decisions, but I seemed to attach myself to guys too easily. They became my world and the cloying part of my behavior chased them away. I knew my faults.

He returned two hours later. I waited, fully dressed, on the couch and stood when he entered. He went to his room, grabbed his sports bag, placed it on the kitchen counter, and walked over to me.

I could actually feel myself trembling and tried to hide my fear behind a stoic expression. Killian's hand came out and hooked behind my neck, jerking me into a hard kiss. Holding my hair and neck, he tilted my head to gain better access. His teeth nipped, and his tongue invaded and consumed more than just my mouth.

I was his.

I sucked in needed air when he finally pulled back all of two centimeters.

"That was not cool. You aren't getting away that easily. Do you get it now?"

I thought it bothered him that Amanda said I had to be in love. He was angry that I thought it would end soon. I couldn't help my relieved smile. "I get it," I said against his lips.

He gave me another mind-blowing kiss that had me rising to my toes before he took my hand and walked me to his car. After he settled behind the wheel, he grabbed my hand and placed it on his thigh keeping it there the entire way to the stadium. Neither of us spoke; Killian needed to focus on his game.

Security waved him through to the underground garage. It was much different than the day I attended the game with my friends. As we walked inside, I could sense Killian was no longer in the same mental realm as me, but he continued to hold my hand until he handed me off to security. No kiss. No hug. Not one word.

Killian was in the zone.

Chapter Fifteen

THANKFULLY, MALORY WAITED INSIDE the skybox. No one else was there. She threw her arms around me and I realized I so needed some form of human connection. She pulled away and we sat down so she didn't need to crank her head back to speak with me.

She wore a different team jersey, not quite as flashy as the one from the previous week, but she still looked gorgeous.

"I can just imagine how being with Killian on your first game day must feel," she said dramatically.

"How do you know I'm *with* him?"

She laughed. "The entire team knows you're with him. Don't be a fool; this is the biggest gossip we have at the moment."

Heat traveled over my cheeks, which only made her laugh harder.

"So why would Killian having a woman with him be gossip? It's more likely him not having a woman would add more to his rumor quota."

Her face took on a secretive look. "Don't get me wrong. Killian dates lots of different women."

My stomach clenched, but she went on.

"What he doesn't do is hide them at his house and keep the team away with death threats."

"Death threats?"

"Yes, silly. He told the guys to back off and stay away until he invited them or he'd do bodily damage. Several of the players work out at his house on Saturdays, including my husband. Now they're nixed until he gives the word. So, tell me, just how good is Football God MacGregor?"

More heat traveled into my face. "You're as bad as Amanda and Lyle."

She gave me a stern look. "That didn't answer my question."

"You're married!"

She laughed again. "Yes, I'm married to a mega-hunk, but really, we're talking about Killian here."

I relented a little. "If we don't count game day, he's wonderful."

Malory stopped laughing. "Game days suck and this is only pre-season. Max doesn't shower until he gets to the stadium no matter how desperately he needs it. He says it's bad luck. In the beginning of our relationship, he didn't want me to shower either." Exasperation showed on her face. "That was an easy one. Hell no! I told him to find a new girlfriend even after he said I could shower in the ladies' locker room here at the stadium." She didn't take a breath before continuing. "Does Killian have any game-day sexual practices I can use to bribe him later?"

The tightening in my stomach had slowly disappeared as she spoke, and my sense of humor returned.

"You mean like whips, chains, and whip cream?"

Malory's mouth fell open and I fought to keep a straight face.

"No, he doesn't do any of those. Yet." I gave her a sly smile.

Her mouth closed. "You're not going to tell me anything, are you?"

"Only that he doesn't talk on game day."

"That's a rough one. Max never shuts up. It's his nerves and game ADHD. He runs around the house a hundred miles an hour. It's actually a relief when we leave for the stadium. If I could convince him that I should drive, I think it would be more survivable."

We talked for more than an hour. A bartender eventually came in and started getting the room ready.

I still had to ask, "Why are we the only two here?"

"Most of the wives and girlfriends sit down in the family seats. When Killian renegotiated his contract, he insisted on seats up here and he lets me use one because he knows Max brings me early. They've been friends since college, so I get a few of the spoils that come with Killian's stardom."

"Amanda and Lyle told me all about your husband when I went to dinner with them a few days ago. I don't think Maxwell Blitz is too shabby."

"Don't get me wrong, Max is one of the best at his position, but Killian is in a different league. He's one of the top players in the NFL, if not number one. Everyone's talking about how he'll do with a real girlfriend for a change."

"I can't believe people already think I'm his girlfriend."

"Wait until the tabloids get ahold of this news. You're still in college, a runner, and a little on the young side. This is going to be fun."

I buried my head in my hands and mumbled, "No fun. It's going to be hell." I lifted my chin. "So how do you know so much about me?"

"I dug deeply as soon as Killian asked me to watch out for you last week." She raised her cell. "Smartphone here. You're on the internet as a runner for the state team. I also saw your high school stats. Pretty amazing, actually."

"In high school, yes, but college is a different story."

"Hey, don't knock yourself. I specialized in chasing boys back in high school, aka cheerleader. I didn't receive a schol-arship and the only school that fell within my budget was a community college. I continued my specialization until I met Max."

Malory was complete cheerleading material. Not that I knocked them. I'd spent countless hours envying their lives. They were short, cute, and never seemed lacking in boyfriends. I wanted to be Malory when I was in high school and a small part of me still did. Killian was changing that. He loved my body, my hair, and especially my long legs.

"What are you thinking about?"

Malory's question brought me out of my daydream and my face flooded with warmth. She gave me a knowing smile.

"Is Amanda coming? I'm going to pick her brain and see if you've given your BFF any inside sexual tidbits I can use."

"You're horrible, you know that?"

"I know but believe me, you'll appreciate my fluff bunny demeanor sooner or later, I promise."

We chatted some more and within a few minutes the owner and his people arrived, followed by my people. Malory was great, but no one replaced Amanda and Lyle.

Amanda jumped up and down, threw her arms around my midsection and her head against my chest. Her height and mine weren't any better a mix than Malory's and mine, but I loved her anyway. Lyle pushed Amanda out of the way and threw an arm around my shoulder.

"How are you, girlfriend?" His exaggerated deep voice made me laugh.

"I'm good and glad you guys are here." I looked at Malory and then back at my friends. "Maxwell Blitz's wife has nothing on the Spanish Inquisition."

"Was she as closed-lipped with you as she was with us?" Amanda asked.

Malory's mouth tipped down in a frown. "Damn, I was hoping you had the goods."

"All I know is that he's hung."

"Amanda Isabelle Frye," I groaned.

"Oops, now I'm in trouble. I swear she would make a better schoolteacher than me. Anytime she uses my full name, I'm on thin ice."

Malory's eyes got big. "Hung, huh? Do tell, please."

Malory looked at me and I looked around to see if anyone was paying attention to my loud-mouthed friends. When I was sure that no one cared, I turned back.

"I'm requesting the family seats next game."

"Yep, he's hung," Lyle said.

I placed my hands to either side of my head and exaggerated pulling out my hair. I'd learned long ago that the best way to get over Amanda and Lyle's gentle teasing was to join in, so I took a breath, lowered my voice, and whispered, "You know why they call Stanley Johnson, Stump?"

My audience's eyes widened.

"They compared him to Killian."

Malory laughed uncontrollably, but when she caught her breath she explained, "I guess the two of you haven't seen Stump's chunk of manly muscle, because really, the guy's a horse." She turned to me and winked. "I'm surprised you can walk."

I was so out of my league when it came to any kind of sexual teasing, so I gave up.

"Please tell me the game is beginning soon."

Chapter Sixteen

Much like the first game, Killian only played until he made a touchdown early in the first quarter. There was no blown kiss this time, and his intensity for the game only seemed to increase. He stood with the head coach talking for the remainder of the first half.

During halftime, I took a walk with my friends to the lower level where we eventually checked out one of the crowded pro-shops. Amanda and Malory talked me into a team jersey with number "twenty" and "MacGregor" on the back. I don't know why I worried, but I couldn't help thinking it might bother Killian.

We made it back to our seats when the third quarter started. When the final whistle blew, I was past ready to see Killian.

He drove the four of us to dinner, and I had no idea where that was going to be until we pulled up at Tillomans.

"You okay with coming here?" he asked.

I didn't have a problem, though as far as my co-workers were concerned, my dating Killian would be out of the bag. I gave him a shy smile.

"Yes, but I hope you made a reservation."

"It's taken care of."

Killian got out of the car and walked around, opening Amanda's door then mine. I'd stayed put until he took my hand and assisted me out. I looked over my shoulder and saw that Lyle had Amanda's hand in his grasp. He winked at me and Amanda smiled.

Sabrina, the hostess, knew Killian on sight and immediately showed us to our table. She gave me a sharp "what-the-hell" look but did her duty with a smile. Our party was slightly underdressed, but Tillomans cared more about their guests having a wonderful dining experience than what you wore. If you could afford the prices, they weren't turning you away.

Killian looked around the table. "I'm hoping everyone here is over twenty-one because I'd like to order a bottle of wine."

I gulped slightly because I knew the wine prices began at more than one-hundred dollars a bottle. Of course, that was if you went for a house wine. Killian didn't. I pulled my big girl panties up and enjoyed dinner and the expensive wine.

"Tell me about your major, Lyle, and what your plans are after graduation."

Lyle began talking about his desire to move to New York, and the college's latest up-and-coming production. Killian focused his attention on Lyle, showing keen interest.

"What did you major in, Killian?" Lyle asked after speaking non-stop for ten minutes.

Killian took a drink of wine before answering. "Entrepreneurial management with a minor in accounting."

I knew about the management, but not accounting. My nemesis is math and I looked at Killian hoping he would tell us more, but our food arrived. Amanda changed the subject and asked Killian football questions between bites.

"So, what do you think the chances are for the Scorpions heading to the Super Bowl this season?"

Killian gave her an indulgent smile. "They're damn good, but anything can happen between now and the playoffs. You intend to place any bets?"

Amanda laughed. "No, I just wondered what you thought since you kind of hold the game in your hands."

I wanted to bury my head. Amanda had decided now was the time to see what Killian was made of. I knew she worked her scheme with my best interest in mind, but doing it here, when he was paying an exorbitant amount for our dinner, wasn't the best time.

Killian didn't miss a beat. "Hmm, I hadn't thought of it quite that way. Before dinner tonight, I was more excited than nervous about the season starting. Now that you've laid the pressure at my door, I'll work extra hard." His face was entirely deadpan for about five seconds.

Amanda's mouth fell open in shock until Killian's dimples flashed. His smile grew and I saw Amanda's eyes go dreamy. I probably had the same look on my face.

A moment later, not having learned from her previous mistake, Amanda made me want to crawl under the table again.

"So exactly what are your intentions for my best friend, besides keeping her hidden away on the weekends?"

I saw Killian's shoulder stiffen for a fraction of a second, but then he relaxed and took my hand, kissing my fingers. His gaze turned back to Amanda.

"Since your best friend considered this nothing more than a fling, I think I'll let her decide where it goes from here."

Amanda didn't blink. "So, you heard that conversation?"

"I heard."

Amanda gave me a look then turned back to Killian. "She tends to think poorly of herself, but I've been trying to break that habit."

Killian cocked his eyebrows. "I'll keep that in mind."

I wanted to run from the restaurant. Killian's fingers were steel around mine, and I knew I wasn't going anywhere. I decided to give her a piece of my mind. "You know, Amanda, your best friend is sitting right here and you are embarrassing her horribly."

"Actually, I find this fascinating," Lyle said.

All eyes turned his way.

He very carefully lay his napkin on the table and fell into a lofty British accent. "I've often wondered how the heterosexual crowd handles jealousy between girlfriends and lovers. The complexities of relationships become quite enthralling when the opposite sex is involved." He looked at each of us and continued while staying in character. "I believe if I was the one who started this conversation, Killian and I would be out in the auto lot discussing the rules of courtship."

Amanda and I were used to Lyle's acting flair and immediately gave our own imitation.

I raised my chin. "Why does each day involve a fight with an American?"

Amanda gave us all a deadpan look. "He's a fortune hunter, my dear, and really, I hate drama."

Killian shook his head. "I think I've lost this round or rather lost my marbles."

Lyle dropped his jaw in exaggerated wonder. "You haven't turned him onto Downton Abbey?"

I looked at Killian. "Sorry, dear, I save Downton Abbey for my best girlfriends."

"I need to go to the parking lot with Lyle and learn the rules," he said. "I don't even know what a downtown abbey is and I have no idea if Rebecca uses it to turn me on or not."

My cheeks went red, but Lyle had broken the interrogation spell and we all laughed.

Killian drove them back to the stadium and they talked football the entire way. I was wondering if there was a Football for Dummies book. If so, I was buying and reading it at the first opportunity.

Chapter Seventeen

"**I** LIKE YOUR FRIENDS," Killian said into the quiet car after making sure Amanda managed to get out of the stadium parking lot.

He squeezed my fingers slightly and then kissed the back of my hand, his lips hot against my skin.

"I'm glad, and very sorry Amanda put you on the spot."

His gravelly chuckle made my thighs clench. "Wait until you meet my mother. She'll know your shoe size within thirty minutes."

"I have big feet, so that's kind of harsh."

"Your feet are perfect, but I agree with Amanda." His grin went a little crooked.

I rolled my eyes. "This can't be good."

"No, I don't think it is. You tend to think poorly of yourself. Mind telling me why?"

Here it was. Our first, in-depth, personal conversation.

I took a deep breath before speaking. "I was taller than anyone I knew by sixth grade. I grew so fast that my coordination didn't catch up fully until around sixteen. I remember falling in the hallway once. My books went everywhere and the kids just laughed. No one stopped and helped me. I ran to the bathroom and cried until a teacher came looking for me." I spoke quickly, took a few deep breaths, and continued. "I hated every day of school, and being incredibly shy didn't help me make friends."

"How tall are your parents?"

I heard sympathy in his voice.

"My dad's tall at six two, but my mom is only five five. She is also one of those butterfly girls like Malory and fits in regardless of the situation. I take after my dad. He's shy with people he doesn't know. I love him because he's a great father and always thought he was the luckiest man on earth for winning my mom."

"I like the sound of that. But butterfly girls? I'd love to hear your definition."

I was looking out the side window then turned his way. "I don't mean it in a bad way. The butterfly girls bloom early. Malory is the perfect example. She's cute, fun, and shines in every situation."

"I don't know if that's totally true. Have you asked Malory about her awkward moments? I think everyone has them."

I tried to keep frustration out of my voice. Killian was gorgeous and might never understand. "You're right. I'm cocoon girl with big feet, and to top it off self-centered. Why don't you give me a few of your inadequacies so I feel better?"

He only took a second before he answered. "I'm grumpy on game day, and don't like my girlfriend saying bad things about herself."

I think my heart stopped for several beats.

"Am I your girlfriend?" I tried to keep emotion out of the question but failed because all the air left my lungs.

This time he brought my hand up and rubbed it against his scratchy jawline. "To me, you're my girlfriend, though that might be a tame word for what I hope we have so far. What am I to you?"

The words tumbled out. I couldn't stop them. "The future father of my children."

Killian gave me a quick glance before returning his eyes to the road. I couldn't believe what he said next.

"That might make up for your uncool words earlier today. Does that line usually scare the guys away?" His voice dropped an octave on the last sentence.

I all but told him I loved him, and I couldn't hold back tears. They slipped down my cheeks, though I fought each one.

"I always scare the guys away," I said honestly. I felt raw, exposed to the point that I wanted to curl into a ball and sob.

He didn't release my hand until we pulled into his garage. I hadn't wiped my face, but most of my tears had dried. I could feel Killian looking at me, but he still didn't say anything. Finally, he got out and walked around to open my door before leading me into the house. It surprised me when he walked to the weight room. About ten steps in, he pulled me against his chest. The warmth of his breath flowed across my cheek.

"I don't know if I'm ready for you to have my babies, but you're not scaring me away, Rebecca Cavanaugh."

My tears began again, but I was solidly against his chest and he couldn't see them. My voice somehow remained calm. "I started dreaming of having your babies on the night we met. Now, we've only been together for a week, but I always latch on tightly. You're my third boyfriend and I did the same thing with the other two. I'm sorry, Killian. I'm only twenty-one, but my biological clock must tick faster than other women."

His rumbled laughter beneath my cheek took me by surprise. He pulled back and turned me around. I stood looking at a floor-to-ceiling mirrored wall. Killian was behind me, his hands resting on my hips. I loved that he was taller than I was.

"Don't move." His low whisper held command.

He left me standing there and walked away. When he returned, he placed my hair up into a hair tie before returning his hands to my hips.

His sculpted arms, holding me, made my insides quiver. I looked up, meeting the chocolate pools of his eyes. I would have turned, but his hands went to the hem of my shirt and pulled the cotton material over my head before I could protest. He dropped it to the floor and unhooked my bra, letting it fall from my body so that I was naked from the waist up.

His hands rose and covered my breasts. My nipples peeked between his splayed fingers while his lips gently pressed against my neck.

"I love these." His fingers flexed in slow, sensual motion.

He continued placing small kisses down my collarbone, traveling behind my neck, and moving to the other side.

"I love your taste."

He slowly released my breasts and moved down to the button on my pants while beginning to alternate his kisses with small nips. I squeezed my thighs together until he pushed my pants over my hips.

"Kick off your shoes." He placed a slightly stinging bite on my shoulder and then another when I didn't immediately follow his order.

My shoes flew a few feet away and he peeled my pants down until they hit the floor. His foot slid between my legs, stepping on my pants, giving me leverage to step out of them. He held me steady as I kicked them off. His lips and teeth continued their magic on every inch of flesh he could reach.

My entire body trembled when Killian's eyes met mine in the mirror. He was so exquisitely beautiful.

"Please take your clothes off, Killian," I groaned out in desperation.

"I will. Later."

His warm hands traveled over the curve of my hips, up my sides and continued back to my breasts, making me clench my legs in anticipation.

"I love these," he said again.

"They're too small." The words came out on a sigh.

"No." He released my breasts, taking my hands and bringing them upward.

It took me a startled second to realize he wanted my hands covering my breasts, but as soon as I did, I tightened my arm muscles and made a sound of protest.

"Trust me, Rebecca. I won't hurt you."

I'd never touched myself with someone watching. It might only be my breasts, but my embarrassment went into overdrive.

He kissed my neck again, whispering, "Trust me."

My arms went lax. His hands covered mine while mine covered my breasts.

"That's how they feel to me. Soft, warm, perfect," he whispered. He accented each word with kisses against my neck and shoulder.

He pulled our hands away slightly and his thumbs came up and slid across my nipples. He used my fingers to do the same. The tips pebbled and my groin pulsed; I needed Killian's touch down there, too.

He released my hands. "Leave them there, Rebecca." His hands moved between us until he cupped the cheeks of my bottom.

"Your ass is so perfect. When you looked for your sister at the party, I stayed just far enough away to watch every sway in that damned skirt. I dreamed about you wearing that skirt and nothing else. I woke up each morning with a hard on that wouldn't stop. I took showers to relieve myself, but nothing helped."

I whimpered and saw Killian smile in the mirror. He moved his hands around until he reached the tops of my thighs.

"God, your legs, Rebecca. I dreamed of that skirt pushed up and your legs over my shoulders while I tasted you. The dream had nothing on that first night you were in my bed.

I could run my fingers along your legs for hours. I think it's turned into a personal fetish."

He pulled back slightly and kissed low on my shoulder while his fingers traveled down the front of my legs. He sank to his knees and his hands never left my body. He leaned to the side slightly so I could see his eyes as they peered into the mirror and traveled upward. I could feel his gaze like a caress.

I studied his face, admiring each sculpted hollow and line. No matter how rugged his features, I found him beautiful.

"You don't get it, do you?" he asked as he kissed the middle of my back.

"Ge, get what?" The tremble running through my entire body made my voice breathy.

"How beautiful you are."

Chapter Eighteen

I WANTED TO BELIEVE him, to erase each insecurity. I wanted to be beautiful for Killian.

His tongue made small circles against my back and then my side as he moved around my body. He was still on his knees and made it look graceful.

"Put your hands on my shoulders and watch the mirror. Keep your eyes open; just watch." His commanding tone held sensual promise.

He lifted my left leg and moved it over his shoulder. I gripped his flesh hard, then harder still when his tongue licked the flesh between my thighs.

"I love the taste of you." He did it again. "I enjoyed spending time with your friends, but god, I wanted to be here, doing this. It's becoming impossible to keep my hands off you." His fingers tightened slightly. "Watch the mirror."

My eyes had drifted down so I had to jerk my head back up. One finger slid inside me, but I couldn't see what he was doing. I felt it. I looked at my flushed face, staring into my own eyes. Killian loved my body. He didn't see the awkward young girl. He thought me beautiful. Tears fell.

"Shh," he breathed against my skin and then added another finger. "Watch yourself come, because with everything I love about you, that's the most incredible. Your face expresses everything I do to you and someday, baby, I'll make you scream."

His lips went back to work, and soon he suckled my clit with noisy kisses and vibrations came from deep in his throat.

The heat built to a raging inferno. Every nerve ending I possessed centered on what he was doing, or so I thought. No, "thought" was the wrong word; I was no longer capable of thinking and rocked my pelvis against Killian's mouth and fingers.

"Come for me, baby. Let me taste more of you."

My cry was louder than ever before. It spilled past my lips as the orgasm burst. My eyes closed and my head dropped back. I rode wave after wave of electrically charged spasms that flowed deeply throughout my body. Before they stopped, Killian scooped me into his arms and carried me to his bed.

The comforter hit my back, and the sight of Killian removing his clothes in the soft bedroom light caused the aftershocks still running through me to go into overdrive.

He came at me from the end of the bed, and before I could protest, I found myself turned onto my stomach. There was no time to worry about being ass up, because his lips traveled up my legs starting at the bottom of my foot. The kisses were like the ones on my neck. Some nice and some stinging little nips of pain that dissolved as soon as his teeth released my skin. I gripped the comforter and held on. He placed one hard bite beneath my left butt cheek then traveled down the opposite leg.

When I squirmed, he held me down with his forearm. I slowly melted into the comforter.

The tug on my ponytail surprised me.

"Up on your hands and knees, Legs."

He guided me up and his warm body covered me from behind. I'd never thought this position could be sexy, but everything Killian did to me was a sensual awakening. He spread my legs farther apart and the slow, hot glide of him pushed through my needy flesh. I couldn't breathe; desire ripped through me. He pulled almost out, but then the heat built again as he slid back in using a slow, steady rhythm to drive me crazy. This time, the orgasm rolled through me in a long sensual wave. When small moans came from my throat, his hands lifted and squeezed my breasts, bringing my upper body from the bed. He pinched my nipples, not hard, but enough to make me cry out. After that cry passed my lips, another followed. His loud groan was next to my ear, his hot breath making me spasm over and over.

I screamed.

We lay in the dark with Killian's arms wrapped around me. He'd turned off the lights and pulled the covers over us. His skin, still slightly damp with sweat, stuck to mine. He removed the elastic holding my hair and tossed it somewhere to the side of the bed. His callused fingers ran through the strands.

I whispered into the quiet room, "I didn't think men liked to cuddle."

He buried his nose against my skin. "After sex, I can smell me," he inhaled again. "On you, and I want you close."

Did he ever run out of ways to make my breath catch? I was so far past being in love with him that the thought of not seeing him for two weeks was almost unbearable.

"What's wrong?"

How did he know?

"I'm going to miss you."

"Come with me for the weekend, I'll arrange the flight. You'll stay in my room and give me grouchy morning sex before the game."

An unladylike snort escaped me. "Grouchy sex?"

"I like you grouchy."

I allowed my Killian MacGregor, after-sex vibe to settle by inhaling and exhaling slowly. "Maybe we should spend some time apart. This is moving fast." I couldn't help but wonder if Killian was speaking in the heat of the moment so I wanted him to have a way out.

His fingers tightened in my hair. "I waited almost two months to see you after that first night. There's been nothing fast enough about getting you into my bed."

Again, that thrill he always made me feel curled my toes. "When are you leaving?"

"I take off on Thursday, but you can wait to leave until after class Friday if you want."

"I need to."

"I'll arrange a flight out for you on Friday evening. That way, you'll be very sleepy and grouchy by the time you get to Washington."

"Is that where you're going?"

"That's where *we're* going."

"You're spoiling me."

"I'm tempting you."

Laughter bubbled over. Killian didn't need to do anything but stand still to tempt me.

"What's so funny?" he growled.

"Everything you do tempts me," I said breathlessly.

He rolled so I lay full-length on top of him. "Then you do the work."

His husky voice was back and I had no problem setting the pace. Killian did though. After just five minutes of me teasing him with the same biting kisses he gave me earlier, he took over.

Chapter Nineteen

HE DROPPED ME AT my apartment Monday morning and another slow week began. It was harder to leave him this time and he didn't make it easier. We almost had sex in his car, in broad daylight.

I went to work Wednesday night and received sly glances from my co-workers. I actually didn't think they expected me to come in. It hurt my pride a little that they would think I didn't need a job just because I was dating Killian.

Thursday night, I was back at my favorite hangout spot with Amanda and Lyle. I remained on the inquisition side while they double-teamed me again.

"You're flying to his game?" Lyle asked in a controlled voice.

"Is there something wrong with flying to his game?"

Amanda took over. "No, nothing wrong, but this is going pretty fast and we're worried about you."

I wouldn't tell them that I said those same words to Killian.

"I'm a big girl and I love you both, but my eyes are open." Liar, liar pants on fire.

They knew better and just looked at me.

"I'm changing the subject now. Lyle, why don't you tell me about your latest boy toy?"

Lyle gave a melodramatic sigh. "His name's Douglas, but he's a little different."

My eyes shifted to Amanda's and she gave me a WTF expression. We turned back to Lyle.

"Different how?" Amanda asked before I could.

"He doesn't do the whole boy-toy thing. He's kind of dominating."

I spit out a small bit of my water, grabbed a napkin, and tried to make myself look less like a fool.

"You're *his* boy toy." Amanda asked, ignoring my behavior.

Lyle turned sideways and gave Amanda his pinpoint stare. "We're working it out."

I'd known Lyle for two years. He was into some kinky sex practices and picked his guys accordingly. From the things he told us, he ruled the bedroom, or dominated it, as he described his sex life.

"Do we get to meet him?" I had to ask. Every so often, Lyle introduced us to one of his special friends if they stayed around for more than a few weeks.

Lyle became interested in what was happening around us, making me feel uncomfortable, so I attacked my other friend.

"Sooo, what about your love life?" I sing-songed at Amanda.

She smiled. "Same old men, different day. Nothing serious and no special news to report. I think I'm jealous of both of you."

"Hell, I'm completely jealous of Becca. All that hot male muscle putting it to her all weekend long," Lyle's voice went dreamy.

Thirty minutes and continued teasing later, I left my friends early so I could pack.

After my two-hour class the following day, I took a little money from my bar jar savings and had myself waxed. Because of the skimpy running shorts I wore during meets, I kept myself well-groomed for track season. Killian hadn't mentioned anything about the hair on my lady parts, but I wanted to do this for him anyway.

The problem was that I always shaved myself with a razor and had no idea what to expect. I was embarrassed and almost lost my nerve before entering the salon. After a short wait, a nice-looking woman dressed in a black shirt and pants took me into a private room. She laid a paper thong on the side table and told me to remove my bottom clothes and dress in just the thong.

"Umm, will a woman be doing this?"

She gave me a sympathetic smile. "First time?"

I gave her a nod.

"Valerie will be your esthetician. She's good and I'll be sure to let her know you're a virgin."

The woman winked at me and left the room.

I changed quickly and then sat on the table feeling like I was waiting for my gynecologist to come in. I'm sure only minutes passed before Valerie stepped into the room, but it seemed like hours. I so wanted this over.

She was professional and asked me about the type of wax I preferred. I decided to go for full frontal nudity. I lay back as she began preparing my skin and I let my crazy mind wander.

Yes, Mom, when I grow up I want to remove shaggy pubic hair from women's bodies. Don't worry, Mom, I'll wear gloves and a mask.

I fought a smile and almost didn't notice when she said, "Ready?"

"Yes."

"Holy fucking hell," I cried out. My upper body came off the table.

She kept her hand pressed firmly against my skin and I knew when she lifted it that there would be no flesh left. How would I explain this in the emergency room?

"I only waxed a small area because it's your first time. Don't worry sweetie, it gets easier." She lifted her hand. There, before my watering eyes, was a hairless strip of red skin. My flesh was still intact, but I didn't think I could take this much pain to my entire pubic area. After several deep breaths, I slowly rested back against the table. There was absolutely no way I could stop now and I kept telling myself that.

I suffered. I cussed under my breath. I about died of mortification again when she waxed between my legs to the back of my vaginal area.

I could hear the class instructor.

We must be sure to wax butt crack hair for the perfect grooming experience.

In zero to thirty minutes, I went from loving Killian MacGregor to hating him for making me think this would add a flare to our sex life. If I wanted a flare, I'd buy one at the local fireworks store and sizzle the damn hair off. It couldn't hurt any worse.

Valerie handed me a nice, folded piece of paper to read about the bumps, redness and ingrown hairs I might experience. Of course, she presented this after she finished torturing me. I had no choice but to accept that I might develop the pussy pox within the next few days.

What the hell had I done?

Chapter Twenty

A DRIVER PICKED ME up from my apartment and drove me to the airport late that afternoon. He handed me my plane ticket and waited while I checked in at curbside. I tried to give him a few dollars.

"Mr. MacGregor took care of everything, ma'am. Have a safe trip."

Killian's money bothered me and I needed to let that negative thought go. I decided to treat this trip like a mini vacation. My parents gave me an iPad as a Christmas gift two years before, so I downloaded the newest book by my favorite author. One of the only things I didn't like about college was the guilt I felt if I read for pleasure. Study, study, study was my mantra.

Of course, Killian bought me a first-class ticket. I felt truly spoiled, and after a brief argument with myself, I again decided to enjoy the experience.

The plane arrived in Seattle late that night. Killian had told me another driver would pick me up at the airport; my heart skipped a beat when Killian stood waiting outside the terminal. He looked delicious dressed in faded denim jeans, dark blue t-shirt, and a baseball cap pulled low over his head.

I noticed people watching as I drew closer. Killian snagged his arm around my waist, grabbed my bag, and kissed me. His taste filled my bloodstream, and I was home.

"Missed you, baby," was all he said after he pulled away much too quickly.

He guided me out of the airport and into a waiting limousine. I saw several flashes before the door closed and the car took off. I didn't have time to process what happened because Killian kissed me properly. He made sure I knew he missed me.

The hotel suite was enormous, but I didn't get a tour because we went straight to bed.

"I need a shower," I managed to get out.

"I need you," he whispered between nipping bites and licks to my neck.

That settled it. A shower could wait. A soft glow of light spilled from the other room, but the bedroom was dark. Our clothes hit the floor and my back hit the bed in record time. He hadn't really touched me yet, but desire threaded through my body, pooling between my thighs in anticipation.

"What the hell?"

Killian's hand had found the part of my body that wanted his touch the most and his voice startled me. Before I knew what he was doing, the bedside light came on and Killian stared at my freshly waxed bare skin.

"Fuck." He drew the word out.

Embarrassment flooded through me and I tried to cup my hands over myself. Killian grasped my hands and pulled them away.

"God, you're beautiful."

His words should have eased my mind, but they didn't. I was mortified.

Killian looked back into my eyes. "This changes things."

"Killian, please turn off the light."

"Why?" He sounded truly perplexed.

"You're embarrassing me."

He moved down the bed and slid between my legs, lifting my ass before placing my legs over his shoulders.

"Stop thinking, Legs."

His warm lips touched my bare folds. I could do nothing but sink my fingers into his hair.

He looked up and said between scrumptious licks, "I like when you pull my hair, I like when you scratch me, but god, Legs, I love when you scream."

And I did. Several times.

I now lay curled with my back against his chest. His fingers trailed from his newest favorite part of me to my knees and back up again.

"Waxing hurt," I said into the quiet room.

His laughter spread his warm breath across my cheek. "I'm surprised you went all the way. I liked you just the way you were, but this is unbelievably sexy." His lips brushed my jaw.

"Like you haven't had bare down there before," I scoffed.

He took his hand from my legs and grasped the back of my head, turning me to look at him. "I've never had you bare down there and that's all that matters. You have the most unbelievable pussy I've ever tasted. I would wade through a forest of hair to get to it."

I giggled. He said the most outrageously perfect things.

I didn't get my shower until the next morning.

After a light breakfast, Killian left for practice at nine. I picked up and folded our clothes from the night before then straightened the suite. The balcony looked over the Seattle skyline. The beautiful city was much cooler than Phoenix, but still not giving into fall gracefully. I decided to read by the pool.

The area was lightly populated, and I had a feeling a few of the women present were football wives or girlfriends. I heard their faint laughter until I became absorbed in my book and the rest of the world went out of focus. A large shadow and then a cool hand on my thigh made me jump.

Killian, freshly showered, and looking good enough to eat, sat down in the chair beside me.

"You're damn hot in that suit, Legs."

I wore a cherry red bikini I'd found on clearance the year before. I preferred a one-piece, but I never had luck finding anything that fit the length of my torso.

His fingers slid under the strip of material at my hip and he leaned in, kissing me deeply.

"Get a room," came from close by. Laughter followed, making me realize several of Killian's teammates were also poolside.

His lips left mine and he whispered in my ear while he nuzzled my neck, "I like their idea, but I want to take you shopping for a dress. We're going out to dinner with Malory and Blitz tonight and I want to buy you something special."

Malory was arriving that afternoon and I was looking forward to seeing her, but I wasn't looking forward to shopping with Killian.

"I brought something that will work for tonight," I said as I placed a small kiss to his chin.

"I'm buying you a dress."

I moved my upper body away so I could look into his eyes. "No, Killian."

His playful look turned serious. "Yes, Rebecca."

He moved back and stood while reaching down for my hand. I made a grab for my cover up, but it slipped through my fingers. He picked it up when I was on my feet and placed it over my head, letting it fall down my body.

"Aw, Killian, my man, don't cover that up." More male laughter along with a whistle punctuated the air.

Mortified, I grabbed my iPad and started back to the room. The cat calls and laughter didn't stop. Had no one ever told him no? He took my hand and tightened his fingers when I tried to wiggle mine from his grasp.

The elevator ride was painfully silent. Looking down at my bare feet, I realized I left my flip-flops behind. As soon as Killian opened the door to the suite, his phone started ringing. I didn't think he'd answer it, because it rang several times, but then I heard, "Hi, Mom." He managed to soften his voice and keep any irritation he felt toward me out of it.

I went straight to the bathroom and successfully closed the door without slamming it. After all, it was Killian's mother on the phone.

I knew I was overreacting and I wasn't sure why. After adjusting the shower's temperature, I stepped in and let the water calm my emotions. My parents worked hard for everything they had. They taught me to do the same. I was proud of what little I'd amassed and prouder still of what I could get by on.

The shower curtain opened and a naked Killian stepped inside. I turned my face to the water, refusing to acknowledge the thrill I felt after a quick glimpse of his body. He pulled me into his chest. The emotional assault I was fighting bubbled over and I started crying. It wasn't pretty.

"Shh, baby, don't cry. I'm sorry." He pulled wet strands of hair from my cheeks. "I won't buy you anything. I promise."

He made me laugh through my sobs. He turned me around and splayed his fingers on both sides of my face. One thumb ran over my trembling lips.

"You are so beautiful."

I didn't argue. There was no point. Killian saw a different me than the rest of the world did. His lips met mine. The kiss was slow and thorough. Deep and all-consuming. He played and teased, leaving me gasping and wanting more. He pulled back and looked at me.

"Better?"

So many things went through my mind. Confusion, need, love. I'm not sure what made me say, "The guy's cat calling and whistling embarrassed me."

He smiled and I touched one of his dimples. I'd wanted to do it for so long. We'd touched each other in such intimate places, but for me this was the most incredible. I don't even think he knew what I did.

"The team thinks you're sexy as hell and that I'm the luckiest man alive."

"You're teasing me."

"No, I teased them. I wanted them to look but not touch them. I don't know if I can stop doing it, but I'll try if it makes you uncomfortable."

I didn't have the heart to burst his balloon. His teammates couldn't possibly think me attractive, but his words still managed to make me feel special. It was impossible to stay mad at him.

"One dress."

I saw the words process and the exact moment he knew he'd won.

"Two."

Thirty minutes later, I agreed. I left the shower cleaner than I'd ever imagined I could get.

"Try on another."

Killian found a boutique on Madison Street that featured clothing for tall women. I knew they existed, but the designer labels were far outside my price range. I had already tried on six dresses. Each one fit better than anything I'd ever worn. I'd never pictured Killian as a shopper, but the man had taste. His whispered words of praise made me blush.

"I like this one." His fingers went to the side slit and grazed my thigh.

I slapped his hand away and he laughed. The clerk winked and I walked back into the dressing room to continue my one admirer modeling gig.

I literally put my foot down when he tried to get me into five-inch heels.

"I'll break my neck. There's no way I'm walking in those."

"What about these?"

They were three inches. Never with another man would I consider them but with Killian by my side, they had potential.

"I'll hold onto you so you don't fall." He added full dimples to the husky words.

In the end, Killian picked a dress that I would wear that evening and another for a future date. Skirts were my thing, but only because I could occasionally find off-the-rack designs that covered my ass cheeks. Dresses never had a long enough waist. These did. The total bill was more money than I made in a month. I managed to accept graciously.

Killian took his time writing something on a piece of paper for the clerk before scrawling his name to the charge receipt, and then we left.

A few hours later, we met Malory and Blitz in the hotel lobby. The men escorted us outside where a chauffeur held the door to a black limousine. Dressed in his dark gray sport coat, Killian took my breath away. His black silk shirt, open at the collar, made me want to lick the exposed skin at his neck. The sleek lines of his pants accented his long legs and even in my three-inch heels, he was tall enough for me to tilt my head back to meet his eyes. I could look at him for hours and never get bored.

Blitz scared me. The man was larger than Killian. His shoulders were so broad I wondered if he had problems fitting through doors without turning sideways. Everything about the man was gargantuan. Next to him, Malory's petite body looked even smaller.

As soon as we took our seats in the limo, Blitz moved Malory to his lap and kissed her. She began running her hands over his chest. I looked at Killian.

He flashed his dimples. "Get used to it. They never stop."

Blitz's laugh filled the interior of the car. "Malory just can't keep her hands off me."

She purred, "That's because there's so much of you and if I don't start now, I'll be up all night trying to touch every inch."

My face was red, but I so wanted to run my hands over Killian's chest.

He pulled me next to him and whispered in my ear, "You can touch all of me later tonight."

I managed to keep my hands to myself and tried my best to ignore where Malory's hands wandered.

The restaurant was wonderful, and even though we were in a rival state, a crowd formed around Killian and Blitz. I practically had to pry my fingers from Killian's grasp so I could step away. He gave me a quick, puzzled look. It didn't matter where we went or what we did, Killian always touched me in some small way. He desired a physical connection and seemed to take hold of my hand subconsciously. He'd done it the first night I'd met him at the party and never stopped. I loved this about him, but at the same time, he needed to handle his fan club without me.

"Blitz doesn't get this attention unless he's with Mac," Malory said quietly as the two men posed for a picture with someone's family.

They signed a few more autographs, and as soon as Killian could make his escape, my hand was surrounded by his once more. He didn't release me when we sat down, and a small, secret grin played on my lips. He never just held my hand, he caressed it; his thumb skimmed across my skin, making me tingle. He would link our fingers then release them, sliding his hand up my arm before returning to my hand. I felt deep down that Killian needed my touch as much as I needed his.

I listened while the men talked football. Apparently, Seattle had a few linemen Killian needed to look out for.

"They're mean fuckheads and won't care that it's pre-season. The best shot they have for the Bowl is to take you out now. The Scorps got your back, but you need to move quickly and make your play. No resting in the pocket. Throw the damn ball out of bounds if you must but keep Blanastovich and Edwards off your ass."

Our waiter interrupted the conversation to take our order. We settled on baskets of crab legs, salad, and Brussels sprouts. I accepted Killian's guarantee that I needed to try the sprouts, and he was right about them. Everything tasted delicious. Killian ordered Quilceda Creek Cabernet

Sauvignon. The men stopped at one glass, but Malory and I finished off two bottles.

It was finally time to leave and I stood from my chair, the room tilted.

"Damn shoes," I muttered under my breath.

Killian stabilized me with an arm around my waist as we walked out to the waiting limousine. Once inside, Malory settled back onto Blitz's lap as I peeked at the shadowed outline of my date. He had his arm around my shoulder while he ran his other hand through my hair. I inched my fingers over his pants to the inside of his slightly spread thighs. His breath caught before he slowly let it out. He didn't stop me, so my moves got bolder. I ran my fingers up and down closer to my goal with each stroke. Finally, I felt the outline of his erection and applied pressure.

Killian's large hand immediately covered mine. "I think you've had too much to drink, Legs."

Though Killian spoke quietly, Blitz heard.

"Fuck, Killian, Malory's already humping my thigh. Do whatever you want, I'm too occupied to check out those legs this time."

Mortification anyone?

Killian's chest rumbled and a playful slap sounded from the other seat followed by giggles and then kissing.

"Just lips, Rebecca," he whispered a split second before his took mine.

My head spun, I moved closer, and before I knew it, Killian hiked me up so I straddled his lap. I didn't care that my back end was on display or that his hands took hold of my ass and adjusted me so I felt the hard push of his erection against my panties. My hands went to his chest so I could unbutton his jacket and slide my fingers inside.

Silk, warmed by his body.

It felt so good against my fingers, but I wanted more. I undid the shirt buttons until my palms rested against bare hot skin. I couldn't get enough and couldn't wiggle much because he dug his fingers into my ass.

Killian threaded his fingers through my hair at the back of my neck and kissed me hard.

I didn't feel the car stop, and suddenly I was sitting next to Killian and he was straightening my dress before he buttoned his shirt. I noticed the same quick manipulation of clothes going on in the seat across from us. Malory let out a very unlady-like hiccup and I giggled. The door opened and Killian unfolded his long legs and assisted me out. We didn't say goodbye to Malory and Blitz, because Killian had me in an elevator before I could catch my breath. My back slammed against the wall and Killian's mouth captured mine. By the time we made it into the room, my dress was unzipped. Within seconds, it, along with my bra and panties, was lying on the floor with me pressed against the door.

Killian fucked me in three-inch heels with one of my legs around his waist and his pants barely past his hips.

The first time.

CHAPTER TWENTY-ONE

I WOKE UP WITH a hangover and no Killian. There were two Ibuprofen along with a glass of water and a note beside the bed.

Legs,

Be back soon. Order yourself breakfast.

K

I placed my order. Killian didn't return until an hour after it arrived. He brushed his lips against my cheek, made his way to the shower, and left me without a word. I'd smelled his sweaty, musky post-workout body. With a smile, I thought that I wouldn't mind if he didn't shower.

When he came out, he turned on the television after sitting on the couch. He didn't look at me or speak.

This was game-day Killian.

I took my shower, fixed my hair and makeup then grabbed my book. A large comfortable-looking chair sat close to the couch, but Killian stopped me before I settled in.

"No. Here." He spread his legs and pointed between them.

I looked at the area he wanted me to occupy and decided to be comfortable. He didn't seem to mind when I sat on the floor and rested my head against his inner thigh. He absently rubbed my shoulders, touching me like always. I relaxed against him and enjoyed every second.

He called Blitz at noon.

"I'm heading out. I'll take a private car. Have Malory collect Rebecca and I'll see you at the stadium."

Killian pulled me into his lap for a kiss, but again it was absentminded.

"I'll see you after the game." He moved me off his lap and stood.

It took him a few minutes to collect his things and then he was gone.

The suite felt incredibly empty without him. I settled on the couch with my book and hoped the time passed quickly.

The game started at six. Malory knocked on the door at four.

I wore my MacGregor jersey and tight jeans. I'd also placed my hair in a ponytail with a large purple bow.

"Now you're getting in the spirit, girlfriend."

Malory was dressed in her sequined Scorpions number six jersey. She handed me a black and purple baseball cap to match hers. I stepped over to a wall mirror and adjusted it on my head. I had no idea what Killian would think of my outfit, but I was ready to sit with the other wives and girlfriends in the stands. We took a private car to the stadium and walked in with the rest of the fans. Green jerseys completely outnumbered our purple ones, but we didn't care.

The excitement in the enormous stadium was exhilarating. The smell of popcorn and hotdogs permeated the air.

"Let's get a dog and drink so we can devour them in our seats."

I hadn't eaten since breakfast and I needed the calories. We waited in line for hot dogs and I heard some whispering behind me. I wouldn't have noticed, but Killian's name came into the conversation.

"Hey, are you Killian MacGregor's girlfriend?"

How the hell would anyone know that?

"Umm, well," I mustered.

"I saw your picture in the paper. He looked really happy to see you at the airport."

"Uh, thank you."

"Are you a model?"

What was wrong with people? There was no way I was model material. "No, I'm a long-distance runner."

"Cool."

We placed our orders and walked to our seats.

"I take it you didn't know you were front page news this morning."

"Front page?"

"There's quite the picture of you and Killian at the airport. Several actually."

"I had no idea. Does Killian know?"

"Not sure, but it won't bother him. It was bound to happen sooner or later. He's never brought a woman to an out-of-town game. Don't get me wrong, there are always available women, and he's hooked up with a few of them, but going to the airport and picking you up was something new for him."

Of course, my mind zeroed in on the "hooked up," but I shook it off. Killian was all mine right now.

Malory introduced me to the players' wives and a couple of their children. With Malory beside me, I felt more comfortable than I had by the pool. They asked me questions about college, and it appeared everyone knew quite a bit about me.

There was a spattering of away fans around us, but mostly we sat in a sea of green. Killian led our team in with boos coming from the entire stadium.

I finished off my hot dog and watched in fascination from my closer seat, which was much closer than the skybox. The noises weren't muted here and I had no idea what I missed by being so far away at the home stadium. The feel of the crowd made the game much more exciting.

The Scorpions received the ball on kickoff. I clapped when Killian ran onto the field, ignoring what anyone might think. He wore a white uniform with purple accents. After two plays, I could tell the intensity of this game was much higher than the first two I'd attended. I heard pads striking pads, grunts, and shouts by fans and players, too. I could see Killian's frustration when an opposing player almost intercepted Killian's pass. His next handoff didn't get the yards needed for a first down, so Killian left the field. I barely watched the game because I couldn't take my eyes off him. He paced back and forth, said something to the coach, and pretty much looked pissed off.

Seattle punted the ball and Killian took the field again. Malory explained play-by-play football terminology to me and helped it all make sense.

On the second play of the next drive, Killian faked a handoff and rolled out to the side. A player in a green jersey took him to the ground with a resounding thud. Killian got up quickly, shaking off an opposing player's hand when he tried to help Killian stand.

The Scorpions came out of a quick huddle. Killian took the snap, went back in the pocket, and threw a long pass. The rest of the fans may have been watching where the ball traveled, but my eyes were on Killian. A hulking figure in another green jersey came out of nowhere and took Killian off his feet. This time his landing sounded more like a crunch and I was out of my seat with my hands covering my mouth. Flags flew up and whistles blew. The Scorpions' number ninety-nine charged the green player as soon as he was off Killian. Number ninety-nine ripped the man's helmet off. Other players joined the fight and fans screamed bloody murder. I only had eyes for Killian, as he lay on the ground barely moving. Several coaches came running and squatted next to him.

"Kick his ass, Stump."

"Late hit. Throw his ass out of the game."

In the back of my mind, I heard the yelling, but I don't think I took a breath until Killian sat up. He didn't immediately get to his feet, but I could see his lips moving while he spoke to the head coach and another man.

"That's Alex, the head athletic trainer. I think Killian's okay, just shook up a bit."

I brought my hands down and clenched them in front of me. The fight had broken up and the referees had the teams separated. The fans quieted and waited. It was another minute before the trainer and coach assisted Killian to his feet. He held his side, but I didn't see him limping. People started clapping and a red-hot anger swelled in my chest.

The referee's voice blasted throughout the stadium. "Delayed hit, roughing the passer, defense number twenty-six, fifteen-yard penalty. After the play was over, unsportsman-like conduct, removing an opposing player's helmet, offense number ninety-nine has been ejected from the game. First down." Cheers rang out from every direction.

My eyes stayed glued to Killian. After he was on the sideline, he bent over and touched his toes, straightened and lifted his arms up, leaned one way and then the other. The trainer continued talking to him.

I turned to Malory. "Who's number ninety-nine?"

"That's Stump."

"He's out of the game?"

"Yep."

"Why isn't the guy who hit Killian out?"

"It's the rules, but he'll be fined between five and ten thousand."

"Dollars?"

"Yes."

"Will Stump be fined?"

"Yes."

Anger settled in my chest because of the stupid rules. "I owe Stump a beer."

"You okay?"

"No, I'll never be okay again." My hands were shaking, and I fought the need to throw up my hot dog.

Malory rubbed her hand across my back. "This is nothing and still pre-season. You'll get used to it."

I finally took my eyes from Killian. "Really?"

"No, not really. But you do get used to your man being bruised, hurt, and sometimes completely beat up. It's part of the game. Football ain't for sissies."

Killian didn't return to the game.

Chapter Twenty-Two

When the game was over, Malory and I returned to the hotel. I didn't feel like having a drink in the bar, so I settled for bottled water while sitting with the other wives and girlfriends. They talked about the game and I thought about Killian.

"I'm going back to my room," I whispered to Malory.

"Okay. I probably won't see you until next week at the opening game."

I went to the suite and walked around, unable to sit still. When the door finally opened, I turned and watched Killian walk in.

"Everything off below the waist. Now."

I stared for a moment.

"Now, Legs. I want you just in my jersey while I fuck you."

"Are you hurt?"

He gave me a frustrated sigh and walked toward me until his chest pressed into the front of mine. His lips were mere inches away. He found the top of my pants, but his eyes stayed glued to me.

"I want to fuck you, Legs, and you're not making it easy."

I threw my arms around his shoulders. Killian's lips slammed into mine, and my jeans and panties were on the floor seconds later. He wasn't gentle.

The first time, he fucked me against the wall and the second bent over the couch. I still wore his jersey, but he managed to slip my bra off through the armholes. I really thought only girls knew that trick, but I wasn't giving Killian enough credit. When it came to fucking, removing my clothes, or making me feel sexy, he was the authority.

When we finally made it to the bed, he nuzzled the hair behind my ear. A sharp, biting sting to my earlobe came next.

"I'm buying more of my jerseys for you, Legs. I saw you in the stands and my cock went hard."

I giggled and slapped him playfully on his chest. "I doubt that, but I don't mind wearing your jersey. I never saw you look into the stands."

"I fight it. I need to stay focused even in pre-season, but I had to be sure you made it to the game."

"Do you always want sex after a game or only when you're hurt?"

"I always want sex with you. Doesn't matter if a game is involved or not."

"Says the man who barely spoke the entire day."

Killian's hand slid through my hair. "It's going to get worse. How do you handle track season? Do you need to find your zone?"

I cuddled closer. "Not like you, but I understand. I tend to be nervous. I think I actually talk more than usual, or at least that's what Amanda and Lyle tell me."

"Hmm." He was back to nibbling on my earlobe.

My hand traveled down his chest until I wrapped my fingers around his cock. It wasn't soft like I expected, but then again Killian's cock was rarely soft. I shifted my body until I could place kisses on his chest. Continuing lower, I slipped my lips around the head and used my tongue. I tasted both of us, and in a million years, I couldn't have imagined enjoying it. My hair fell forward and Killian gathered it, lifting it out of the way. I gazed up and his brown eyes drilled into mine. He held my head still and pushed farther into my mouth.

"What can you take, Rebecca?"

I didn't answer, just closed my eyes, loosened my throat muscles, and took his cock deep.

"Fuck."

And I did.

We barely slept that night. I woke up the following morning feeling decidedly achy in all the right places. Black and blue bruising covered Killian's lower side and I forgot my small discomfort.

"Don't worry about it, Legs. Just bruising."

"How do you know?" My anger at the Seattle player rose again.

Killian kissed my fingers and placed them against his injury. "Because I've had broken ribs before and this is nothing. I know I would feel better if you kissed them all better, though."

How could I resist his dimples?

Malory and I left on the same flight. Team rules dictated that the players fly back together. I had homework and I needed to pick up notes from the class I missed. Killian wasn't happy, but I needed to be at my apartment that night, not in his sexy arms. I called a fellow college teammate and we ran together after the sun went down. I fell into bed exhausted but was unable to fall asleep.

My phone rang and I smiled at the display.

"Hi," I said dreamily.

"What are you doing?" His husky voice made my toes curl.

"Lying in bed thinking of you." I smiled against the phone.

"You should have stayed the night and you'd feel me slide between your thighs right now." There was gentle chide to his voice.

"Hmm, I'd be digging my nails into your back." I squirmed and fought putting my hands where I wanted Killian's cock.

"Touch yourself."

"Killian!"

"Touch yourself, Rebecca. One finger, just the tip. Run it over your clit."

How could I resist his voice?

His tone lowered another octave. "Now slip your finger inside your pussy." He breathed in and out so I could hear. "Is it there?"

"God, Killian, I need you."

"My hand is wrapped around my cock, pumping up and down, but in my mind, I'm fucking you. Add another finger but go slow."

I breathed more harshly into the phone.

"You still there, Rebecca?"

"Yes, Killian."

"Then come open this damn door so I can fuck you the way I want."

"I'm going to kill you," I said as I jumped from the bed and ran to the door and threw it open.

"Fuck me first," he demanded, and ground his lips against mine.

My exhaustion melted away.

Chapter Twenty-Three

THE FIRST REGULAR SEASON game was the following week and it was at home. There was a completely different vibe of excitement in the air and Killian's intensity doubled. I somehow resisted the urge to throttle him the day of the game. I tried to understand but couldn't help feeling I would be better off at my apartment while he did his intense indifference to me being with him thing. The Scorpions won, and Killian's after-game sex almost made up for my trampled feelings.

During the week, I immersed myself in classes, homework, and Wednesday night waitressing. Somehow, the media got wind that I worked at Tillomans and my boring weekday life became social media fodder. My manager didn't mind, but I found it difficult to field questions from sports reporters and do my job.

Campus life wasn't much better. Students pointed me out and brave ones asked me about my relationship with Killian.

"Is it true? What's he like in bed? What did you do to rope him in?" were only a few of the questions I dodged. The guys didn't approach me, but their assessing gazes made every step I took a challenge. Falling on my face was a real possibility because of the stress I felt.

"Sorry, babe, it goes hand in hand with my life. Quit your job and stay here Wednesday nights," Killian said when I told him about work.

"I need the money, Killian." I rolled over and placed my finger against his lips. "Don't say it."

He bit my finger and didn't let it go.

"No, Killian."

He rolled and had me beneath him, raising my hands above my head. "I hate when you tell me no."

I couldn't help laughing. "You hate for anyone to tell you no."

"It's not something I hear often, but with you it's especially irritating."

"Get used to it."

"Hmm." He tickled me until I begged him to stop.

I didn't quit my job.

The second week of regular season was another home game, which they won. The Scorpions hit the road for their next game. I couldn't go because I needed to complete a research project. Killian gave in grudgingly. We'd never discussed him hooking up with another woman after an away game and it ate at me during the weekend. He called Saturday night, sounding lonely, which made me feel better.

I didn't hear from him again until Sunday after his game. We talked for more than an hour. I slept that night knowing Killian missed me and was flying in late to sleep alone in his bed that night. I didn't discuss my insecurities with him. I knew he wouldn't like my thinking.

The following week the team had a Monday night game, and then the Scorpions had a bye week. If I thought the excitement in the stadium amped up when regular season started, it was nothing compared to Monday night. By now, I'd ordered and read a copy of Football for Dummies, and didn't need Malory to give me a play-by-play anymore. When Killian's teammates came over to his house, I kept up with conversations, though I didn't impart any wisdom on the subject.

I still wasn't accustomed to the minor injuries Killian suffered, but I learned to keep my feelings to myself and kiss him all better.

The Monday night game started well but progressively turned sour. By the end of the first half, the Scorpions were down by a touchdown, and I was getting nervous. Fights broke out in the second half and the Scorps lost by ten. To top it off, Killian threw two interceptions.

"Good luck," Malory whispered to me before we went to the locker room.

Killian had promised to get me home before my Tuesday morning class, and without a word, he drove me to my apartment. I knew he was disappointed and angry, but his refusal to verbalize his feelings pissed me off. I didn't wait for him to come around and open my door. I heard him following me to my door. He took the key out of my hand and opened it, still without a word.

"Killian, just go home," I said when he closed the door behind us.

His fingers sank into my hair and his lips came down. If he wanted to punish me for his loss, the kiss did just that.

Without really knowing what happened, I was on my knees while Killian unzipped his pants. He fucked my mouth, carried me to my bed, kissed my cheek and left.

I cried for an hour.

He didn't call Tuesday night, and I fell asleep on a wet pillow. Killian MacGregor was an ass.

On Wednesday, I arrived at work and started my shift with a heavy heart.

Sabrina walked up to me, "Sorry, honey, but it looks like your ex-boyfriend is here."

My ex? What the hell? Why would she say something like that? She didn't know my ex-boyfriends.

I turned and Killian was holding out a chair for a woman; all I could see was the back of her long brown hair.

Sabrina continued, "He specifically asked for one of your tables and there was nothing I could do. In my opinion, the woman is too old for him, but not my problem."

My heart was lost somewhere in my lower stomach. I really thought I was going to be sick. I squared my back, didn't say a word to Sabrina, and walked over to confront Killian. I would probably lose my job, but I was past caring. The son of a bitch didn't speak to me for two days after a blow job and then showed up with another woman where

I worked. I planned to leave his body with more than a few bruises.

Killian saw me walking toward him and stood. His lip quirked slightly, but his dimples barely showed. He was nervous. He damn well should be. His hand came out, but I ignored it. I only needed to be close enough to damage his face, and then I was leaving.

"Mom, I'd like you to meet Rebecca."

Startled, I turned to Killian's...date. Her smile was her son's smile, though other than her lips and dimples, they looked nothing alike. She was beautiful, appeared years younger than she had to be, and I was going to murder Killian MacGregor.

"Hi, dear. Please call me Beth. Killian has told me so much about you."

I shook her hand, turned slightly, and gave Killian my best killing glare and calmly asked if I could get them an appetizer.

Confusion showed clearly on Beth's face.

"Sorry, Mom, but Rebecca just survived her first game loss and I owe her an apology."

"Oh, well then, I understand. I need to find the ladies' room and that will give the two of you a chance to talk." She gave me a hesitant smile and walked away.

The tables near us were not occupied, though it wouldn't have mattered. I turned the full force of my anger on my ex-boyfriend.

"What the fuck are you doing, Killian?"

"My mother wanted to meet you."

I took a slow, calming breath hoping I wouldn't start crying. "And I wanted to hear your voice, talk to you, make sure you were okay. But no, you got your suck off and gave me the fuck off. How dare you show up here tonight with your mother."

I was impressed that I managed to keep my voice relatively low.

I saw a touch of anger spark in Killian's eyes. "I told you what being with me was like during season, Rebecca. I don't like to lose."

"You know what, Killian, that's just too damn bad. I'm sorry your tricycle got mangled and messed up the shiny red paint. I'm an adult. I don't like to lose either, but I would never do what you did."

Killian's eyes went over my shoulder and I knew his mother was standing behind us.

I moved slightly so she could sit down in her chair.

"I'm sorry, Mrs. MacGregor, but my break is starting and I won't be available to serve your meal."

I walked away and didn't look back. I made it past the kitchen into the back storage room before I started crying. Jim, my manager, came in. He was obviously at a loss, but agreed to have another waitress cover my tables. I slipped out the back door and made it home to my apartment in one piece.

I couldn't stop the flow of tears and had no idea what time it was when someone pounded on my door. It didn't take much imagination to figure out it was Killian. I walked to the door, refusing to open it, and childishly told him to go home.

"I'm not going home, Rebecca. Open the damn door."

Maybe, I thought, we needed to end this here and now. I opened the door and stepped back.

Killian walked in and turned to face me. I closed the door behind him with a resounding thud.

"I'm sorry." His eyes showed so much hurt.

I hated myself for wanting to give in and melt against him so badly, take him in my arms and kiss him until sometime tomorrow. But I knew our relationship wasn't going to work.

"I know you're sorry Killian and I'm sure you'll be sorry the next time and the next. I can't deal with your single-minded intensity for the game. I've thought about it. You make me feel beautiful and I have more confidence in myself than I've had since I was twelve years old." I took a calming breath before continuing. "But, Killian, you've hurt me more than anyone ever has. I'm not pro-sport girlfriend material. I'm middle of the pack and happy to be there. Go home, Killian, and thank you for everything."

He just stared at me and I could feel my eyes welling over. I didn't want to cry in front of him, but I knew it was pointless to think I could hold them back. I moved away from the door hoping he would leave.

He took a step closer, but didn't touch me. "I love you, Rebecca."

I closed my eyes.

"Please don't cry." Fingers brushed the side of my face. "I didn't mean to hurt you, but I shut down. I was just going to drop you off at your house, not touch you, but I couldn't help myself. I'm a fucking bastard, but, baby, I love you."

I leaned forward just a bit and I was in his arms. God, I loved him, and at the same time felt a crushing pressure inside my chest. Killian picked me up and carried me to the couch.

"I love you," he said over and over, smoothing my hair away from my face, making me cry harder.

His lips finally rested against my forehead for a moment before sitting me against the couch cushions and walking away. He came back with a box of tissues. When he tried to blow my nose, I grabbed the tissue out of his hand and did it myself.

I managed to gain control, but I needed him to know how I felt. "I can't do this again, Killian." I looked up at him and saw the hurt I felt reflected in his eyes. "I love you, too, and that made this so much worse."

He kissed me. It was soft and sweet and full of promise. His arms went around me and he pulled me tight against his chest. "My mother wants you to come over for dinner this Sunday."

"Your mother hates me."

His chest rumbled and I clenched his shirt.

"She doesn't hate you. The woman won't come to any of my games. She doesn't put up with me after losing or even before a game when I won't talk. She told me years ago she'd knock my head into the nearest wall for my attitude if it didn't change. When I was in high school, she made me clean our apartment on game days. I'd scrub the bathroom floor on my hands and knees and she'd point out every spot I missed."

I was laughing now. "I don't think your sports psychologist is working very well, Killian."

His hand tightened in my hair. "He is. You have no idea how bad things used to be."

I pulled away and looked into his eyes. "Make love to me. Please don't fuck me."

I didn't need to say anything else. Killian carried me to the bed and slowly took my nightshirt and panties off. He stood and removed his clothes. When he leaned down on the bed, his hands and lips worshipped my body. I kissed him whenever I could reach skin.

The slow build of my orgasm made me gasp for air. Liquid heat pooled between my legs as his fingers worked their magic. I burned until the spasms overflowed. Killian's eyes found mine and his cock met my still-quivering entrance.

"I love you, Rebecca." He slid inside.

I watched him move; his hair partially covered his eyes and his lips drew into a firm line. He moved in and out with slow, measured strokes. The heat built again, or maybe it had never stopped. Killian gritted his teeth when my next orgasm shook throughout my body, but he didn't stop.

"Please, Killian."

"I love you, Rebecca." His thrusts became harder, his breath more ragged.

I cried out when my body tightened again and this time he groaned loudly. Killian succeeded in making me feel loved.

But I still knew it wouldn't last.

Chapter Twenty-Four

I WOKE UP EARLY with small kisses on my shoulder.

"Mmm." It felt too good to articulate more.

"Can I fuck you now, Rebecca?" Killian's warm breath brushed across my ear.

"Yes, please."

And he did.

Twice.

I came out of the bathroom knowing we needed to begin our day, but his open arms were too inviting, so I crawled back into bed.

"Can we talk about what happened after my game?" Killian asked after he tucked me in close.

My body immediately stiffened. His fingers slowly smoothed over my skin until I relaxed.

"Something comes over me when things don't go right on the field. I know you don't want to hear excuses, but please listen?" He gave me time to object, but I didn't say anything. "Most of the women I'm with are only around for a few weeks at most. I've always just wanted someone to fuck with no emotional commitment. I've had women in the locker room after a loss. I've never driven them home or brought one back to my house. They meant very little to me, and as you know, I'm not easy to be around when I fuck up in a game. I'm not proud of my behavior with women, but I owe you the truth."

I controlled my breathing. I didn't want to hear this.

"I don't want to feel the way I have the last few days. I would rather not see you on game day or after a loss," I said gently.

"Come to my mother's house for dinner next Sunday, please?"

He wasn't giving me answers, but I had no fight left. He'd loved most of it out the night before and managed to fuck away all but a few lingering doubts this morning.

I didn't want to face his mother, but what could I do? "I'll come to dinner."

"And spend the weekend with me?"

"Yes and spend the weekend with you."

Killian let out a long breath. "I need to get home and grab my stuff for practice."

"Okay." I tried to keep the sadness out of my voice, but it didn't fool him.

"May I spend the night tonight?"

"Yes." I gave him a sweet smile.

I watched him dress. His kiss before he walked out the door was much too brief. Sexually frustrated, I lay in bed for another ten minutes before I went for my run. It was later than I liked and heat rolled off the cement, but I needed my running high.

Killian spent the night Thursday then picked me up on Friday. It was his bye week and he acted more relaxed than he had since the season started.

"I want to take you out to dinner." His eyes traveled over my body like he hadn't seen it in weeks instead of hours.

My inner thighs ached and I clenched them tightly, noticing Killian's smile when I did it.

"Someday I'll cook for you, but yes, I'd love to go out."

We stopped at his house so he could change into something more formal and I could put on the other dress he bought me in Seattle. I looked in his closet and saw more than the dry-cleaned dress I already wore and the one I planned to wear tonight. All of them were there. Each dress I had tried on in Seattle.

"Killian."

His arms closed around me, his lips feathering kisses across my neck. "I love you and that means I can buy you things. Wear the one with the high slit on the side."

"I hate you."

"No, you love me."

"You cannot buy me things."

He turned me and tipped my chin up. His sexy dimpled grin made me dizzy. "Can too." The childish words were incredibly sexy with his deep voice. I fought my smile, but it escaped right before he kissed me.

I wore the indecent dress with the side slit and blushingly put up with Killian's roving hands the entire night.

It was the best weekend Killian and I had spent together. He was loving, fun, and just about fucked my brains out. But that was all before we went to his mother's.

She greeted us at the door of a beautiful house in a large, sprawling neighborhood in Glendale. Orange trees peppered her property and it seemed immensely cooler than the section area where I lived. Not as much asphalt, I guessed.

This time she pulled me into her arms for a hug. "Thank you for forgiving my son. Maybe you should have held off another week. It would have served him right. Beat him over the head with a frying pan if he pulls his game-loss pouty behavior again."

Killian kissed his mother's cheek. "Thanks, Mom. I know I can always count on you."

She laughed and I saw her "Killian" dimples again. Or, I guess, Killian's were "Beth" dimples.

"Your brother knows you're coming and he's excited. Go visit while I talk to Rebecca."

Killian looked over his shoulder as he walked from the room. "Remember, Amanda? Shoe size?"

I blushed.

Killian laughed and continued down the hallway. I'd forgotten about his brother. I had no idea how old he was, but I guessed still young enough to live at home.

"Come on, dear. Ignore my son. I'm so glad you're here. I'm preparing dinner, if you don't mind keeping me company."

"Thank you, Mrs. MacGregor."

"Beth."

"Thank you, Beth."

The kitchen was enormous and just as lovely as the rest of the house.

"Killian picked this house out for me because of the kitchen. I'm sure you know by now that he can't boil water. Have you met, Marty, his chef?"

"No, he and I seem to miss each other." I blushed again. I'd almost said I was only at Killian's on the weekends.

Beth didn't seem to notice. "I stopped going to Killian's games years ago. It was too hard to work out scheduling details when he played in college. Then after he went pro, too brutal. I can't handle seeing someone cause my son pain. You know tennis would have been the perfect sport for him."

I had to laugh.

"My son tells me you're a runner."

"Yes, ma'am. I run for the state team."

"With a scholarship and everything." She gave me a proud look that took me by surprise.

"Yes, I was lucky back in high school."

"I know that's a lie. Colleges don't give scholarships because of luck." She didn't let me argue. "So do you plan on staying in the valley after college?"

"Yes, my parents live here, and my sister."

"Oh, Killian didn't mention you have a sister."

I blushed again. Like I would explain how Killian and I met. Not! "Killian didn't tell me about his brother either," I said to change the subject.

The look on Beth's face changed and a bit of anger flashed in her eyes. "I'm sorry. You need to meet Michael, he'll be joining us for dinner. I'll have a few words with my son on the phone this week and clear up his future problems in regard to the subject of Michael."

I had no idea what I'd walked into, but it wasn't good.

"Come on and I'll make introductions. His nurse will be here this evening, but for now we're on our own."

I followed Beth as she walked with purposeful strides to the back of the house. I heard Killian's voice as we drew closer to the door.

Using a tone I'd never heard before, he said calmly, "You're going to love her, buddy. She's tall and beautiful—"

Killian looked at Beth and me when we walked in. My eyes went to the wheelchair where Killian's brother sat with a blanket on his lap. His small, thin hands curled unnaturally in front of him. His head was propped up by a brace at the top of the chair. His lips tilted downward. He watched Killian but attempted to turn our way when Beth spoke. Killian stood, shifting the chair slightly.

"Michael, this is Rebecca, Killian's friend." Beth's voice was soft.

Michael made a small, inarticulate noise and I could do nothing but smile. At the same time my heart broke. This was Killian's brother and he'd never told me anything about him.

"I was just giving Michael the low down on my girlfriend and hadn't gotten around to the good parts yet."

"And you won't, Killian Allan MacGregor," Beth snapped, though she smiled at the same time.

"I wasn't going into full detail. I wanted to tell him about her blue eyes, long legs, and grouchy behavior when she's tired."

Killian loved his brother. It was obvious, but I couldn't help feeling left out because he hadn't said a word about Michael.

"I'll finish cooking and leave you to become better acquainted." Beth walked out.

"Sit here, Rebecca, and I'll turn his chair so he can see us both."

I sat on the bed, Killian turned the chair, and Michael became animated.

"He wants you to hold his hand."

I leaned forward and put my fingers over Michael's. They were cold, but he stopped fidgeting as soon as I touched him. His lips tilted just slightly into what had to be a grin.

"I told you you'd like her, buddy."

"I like you, too, Michael." How could anyone not?

"I need to catch him up on my games."

Killian began a play-by-play of his last two games. The first was easy because he won, but I heard his voice tighten when he talked about his loss. The smile left Michael's face and he seemed to understand Killian's pain over losing.

"That son of a bitch sucker punched me in the pileup, but Blitz took him down on the next play."

Killian didn't leave anything out. He told about his good plays and the interceptions.

"Next week, we're out of town." Killian talked until his mother came in and told us dinner was ready. He pushed Michael's chair to the empty spot at the table. Michael wasn't fed; Beth explained he ate through a feeding tube.

"He likes to sit in here with us. He has two nurses that take revolving shifts, but Sundays they take off until the evening. It's nice when football is in off-season because Killian eats here on Sundays and helps me out."

Seeing Killian's family was eye opening. No one mentioned his father, but seeing the three of them together, I felt the love they shared. My emotions were a jumbled mess by the time we said goodbye.

Killian MacGregor had some explaining to do.

Chapter Twenty-Five

THE CAR REMAINED DEATHLY quiet on the trip back to Killian's house but he held my hand like he always did. We pulled into his driveway and he hit the button for the garage.

"You okay?"

I turned. "I'm not sure."

"I'll let you out and we can go inside and talk."

We needed to talk. About many things. I had spoken to Killian about my parents and sister. He listened but had offered very little about his personal history. This was so wrong.

I followed him, my hand held tightly in his grip. He sat on the couch and brought me into his side.

"You're angry that I didn't tell you about Michael?" His voice was whisper soft.

I looked at the pain in Killian's eyes. "I'm not angry, I'm hurt. Why didn't you tell me? Did you think I'd react badly? Did you think I'd have a problem with your brother's disability?" I couldn't go on because anger was slipping into my voice.

"God, no," Killian said while pulling me closer. "It's difficult for me to talk about Michael. I knew you would care about him as much as I do."

I felt tears behind my eyes.

"Then why?"

"Because it's painful."

He wasn't saying more, so I needed to move this farther along. "How old is Michael?"

"Twenty-five. He was born on March sixteenth."

Fuck. Killian's birthday.

"He's my twin brother."

Michael had the body of a twelve-year-old. He couldn't talk or move his arms more than a few inches. Shit, the first tear slipped down my face. Killian kissed it away.

"What happened?"

I watched Killian's chest expand as he took in a large supply of air.

"Michael was the troublemaker of the two of us." Killian's dimples flashed. "I know that's hard to believe, but even my mother will back my story. We vacationed at a cabin on the river when we were nine. My parents saved money for two years so we could have that one special week. There were rocky cliffs several hundred yards away that partially circled a swimming hole. A large sign with, "Danger, no jumping," printed on it signaling the danger. My dad told us he would skin us alive if we jumped from those cliffs."

Crap, my heart took a plunge because I knew what was coming.

"At around five on the first morning, Michael woke me up and dared me to jump off the cliffs with him. I usually got my ass tanned right along with him because I never refused a dare and he knew it. The sun was barely up and my parents were sleeping. I was scared. I remember looking at that sign and thinking we shouldn't jump. But we did."

Killian looked away from me and I squeezed his hand. When he glanced back, there was so much pain. I felt more tears slip down my face.

His voice was choked. "I came up and Michael didn't. At first, I thought he was playing a practical joke, but then I knew something was terribly wrong. I started diving under and searched for him. I'd come up for air and scream for help then dive back under. The water was so dark, but finally I touched him and tried to pull upward. My lungs almost burst and I had to breathe. I let him go and went up for air, leaving him down there. I made it down to Michael again, and my dad was finally there helping to pull him up. He was completely blue when he came out of the water. My dad started CPR and my mother helped. I sat next to him, holding his lifeless hand, begging him to come back."

A sob escaped my lips.

"Shh, baby, don't cry." Killian pulled me in even closer and rocked me in his arms. "It happened a long time ago. My mother and I survived. My father left a year later. He couldn't take the pain of seeing Michael every day. He never blamed me, but I know he blamed himself. Michael was on life support for months. My father wanted the machines turned off, but my mom refused."

There were so many things going through my head.

Killian holding my hand and his subconscious desire to touch.

A nine-year-old child faced with death or letting go of his brother.

Killian's childish insecurities and even his anger.

It all made sense now, and, god, I loved him.

We stayed locked together until we changed our position and settled full length on the couch. Killian spoke about his brother before the accident. One scrape after another. Two boys completely inseparable. He made me laugh in between more tears. Killian's mother was simply amazing.

"I had to support them. I needed to play professionally so Michael and my mom would always be cared for. I had to complete each pass, make every touchdown, and win games. There was no other option."

This was such a different picture than what I woke up with this morning.

"Has Michael ever gone to any of your games?"

"I've never tried. He doesn't do well in crowds. But he gets excited watching football on television. I had the sky-box seats put in my contract in case he could come someday. I'm just afraid of what would happen, and I couldn't ask my mom to bring him. She worries about me too much and doesn't enjoy watching. Most of my teammates have met Michael at one time or another. I don't keep him a secret, but they're guys and don't ask the hard questions. I needed to tell you everything."

"Thank you."

"It's also the reason it took almost a month to contact you after we met. Michael was in the hospital because of a respiratory infection."

Things. It wasn't another woman; it was Michael.

Killian kissed the top of my head. "I'm worn out. Let's go to bed."

He made love to me. If I thought Thursday night was mind-blowing, I was wrong.

Tonight, Killian MacGregor rocked my universe.

Chapter Twenty-Six

The following weekend, Killian refused to take no for an answer, so I flew into Dallas for his game. By now, I had several number twenty jerseys in home and away colors. I followed what happened on the field like a pro, but still had trouble watching Killian get tackled or sacked, as the case was in the second quarter. Killian got up instantly then threw a touchdown on the next play. Scorpions won thirty-two to fourteen.

The following week was a home game. Malory and I opted to sit down with the other wives and girlfriends. This allowed us to be obnoxiously loud and I discovered what a great cheerleader Malory actually was. I found myself watching our antics a time or two on the big screen and wondered if Killian saw us, too. The Scorpions won seven six, but Killian didn't play well. I could see the fury rolling off him in waves by the end of the game and realized I needed to stay at my apartment that night.

He pulled me close in the locker room before we walked to his car. It surprised me when he drove to his house.

"I don't mind going home, Killian," I said when I figured out where we headed.

"You're coming home with me."

"It's probably not a good idea." I kept my voice even.

He didn't say anything until we walked through his front door. "I'm grabbing a beer and heading to the pool. Join me if you want."

Hmm, let's see. Go study for a coming test or spend an hour with a silent jackass. I chose to study. I actually made it thirty minutes before I couldn't take it. I needed to know that he was okay.

Grabbing a beer, I headed outside. Killian's powerful arms ate up the pool, lap after lap. I still wore my clothes, so I just dipped my feet in the water and watched. I had no idea how much time passed, but eventually Killian swam toward me and came up between my legs, dripping water.

"Hi," I said shyly.

He didn't answer, and before I knew what happened, I was submerged in the pool gasping for air when my head came out of the water.

"You dirty rat bastard," I yelled.

"I love you." His cold lips settled against mine.

The kiss went on and on. He removed my pants, which wasn't easy because they were wet, and slipped his cock inside me straight to where I needed it most. I wrapped my ankles around his waist, sinking my fingers tightly into his hair. This sex was somewhere between fucking and making love. I didn't care which; I was just glad he responded.

After our breathing settled, Killian pulled me to the steps, arranging me between his legs. I leaned back into the warmth of his chest. It wasn't cold, but a gentle wind blew across my wet body causing goose bumps on my arms. Killian wrapped himself around me and took away the chill.

"I sucked today."

I wasn't sure how to answer his statement. This was unchartered territory for me, so I just cuddled closer and squeezed his arms.

"Nothing fucking went right. I just wasn't on my game. I didn't feel it."

I leaned away, turning slightly, and kissed his stubbled jaw.

"We have one of our best chances to get into the Super Bowl this year and we need me at my best."

There was no way I was reminding him that the Scorpions won. I just continued kissing his chin and jaw, the side of his neck, his shoulder.

A small tug on my hair stopped me.

"Are you even listening to me?"

"Of course, I am." I went back to kissing and nibbling.

"You." He tugged my hair again. "Are not listening."

"You didn't feel it. Go on. I swear I heard every word." His chest rumbled against me and he laughed.

"I love you," he said.

"You said that already."

"Not nearly enough, baby. Thank you for being here."

"You didn't give me a choice."

"You made the choice when you came into the locker room." He pulled my hair back so my neck was in the path of his teeth.

"I don't have all the Killian game day rules down yet." I groaned when he gently sucked on the skin he just bit.

"Are you giving me a hickey?"

"You gonna stop me?"

I turned in his arms and attacked him low on his neck. If he could mark me, I could damn well return the favor.

"Come on. We're finishing this discussion in bed."

"Do I get to hear more about how bad you sucked today?"

"No, baby, I get to feel how hard you suck today."

"You have such a golden tongue," I said with delight.

"God, I want to spank you."

"Not if you want to see how hard I suck." I broke away and made a run for the house. I knew he waited to pounce until I was near the bed, but I still squealed.

"Scream for me tonight, baby."

I looked deeply into his intense dark eyes. "Make me scream, Killian."

He did.

CHAPTER TWENTY-SEVEN

KILLIAN MET MY PARENTS on Thanksgiving. Candi barely spoke to me. She'd called a few times to get the inside scoop on Killian and I'd cut her short. She had no problem pointing her flirtatious endeavors Killian's way, though. She was a seriously embarrassment. At the same time, I had her to thank for placing me in Killian's path. But there was no way I was telling her that.

"Are you in college?" Killian tried very hard to be polite.

"No, my sister got the brains. I've got other specialties."

Killian didn't bat an eye, but he didn't ask what those specialties were either. Candi didn't like it when her sexual enticement skills didn't work. She went into a full-blown pout and didn't speak for several blissful minutes. Unfortunately, it was short lived.

"So, are you friends with Lenny Brower?" she asked in her sweet but bitchy voice.

"I'm friends with all my teammates." Killian glanced at me and gave my hand a small squeeze under the table before turning back to my sister.

"He and I are rather close. He says you've been known to party at his house on occasion."

Killian's tone remained even, but I caught a subtle change. "It's been a long time and I don't see myself there again in the near future."

"I'll tell him you said that."

Killian smiled. "Yes, please do."

Though Candi no longer embarrassed my parents, I was grateful when my mother broke in and asked Killian about his college days.

My mom and dad were good people and it gave me a warm feeling knowing they liked Killian. He and my dad watched a football game on television while my mom, sister, and I cleaned the kitchen.

"I'd like to help, Mrs. Cavanaugh," Killian said, but my mom shooed him away.

I smiled because I already knew there was no chance a guest would help with kitchen cleanup. My sister pounced as soon as the swinging door to the kitchen shut.

"You think you're all high and mighty now that you've roped in a star quarterback?"

I'd never stood up to my sister, but Killian had given me confidence in myself that was never there before. "He's not a quarterback. He's THE quarterback, or don't you read the sports page?"

"I hope you left off using birth control so you can keep him."

"That's enough, Candi." My mother's voice was sharp.

I didn't bother to answer Candi's taunt, because she was trying very hard to get a rise out of me.

My mother put her peacekeeping abilities into play. "So does Killian's family live here?"

"Yes, his mother and brother live in Glendale."

"Killian has a brother?"

The glee in my sister's eyes made me laugh. "Yes, he has a brother. His name is Michael, and he's Killian's twin."

"Shit, Killian MacGregor has a twin brother. Is he as good looking as Mac the Knife?"

"Actually, I think he's cuter."

"I hope you plan on inviting his mom and brother here to dinner sometime soon," my mom said.

"Yes, I'd love to. Maybe after the playoffs. Killian's traveling schedule is pretty hectic over the next two months, but I'll arrange something as soon as I can."

"Yes, sister dear, please arrange something. He's not married is he?"

God, Candi was awful. "No, he's not married." I knew it was spiteful of me and Michael didn't deserve my sister's obvious scheming, but she was on my last nerve. She always brought out my bad side.

Killian and I escaped at halftime. We drove to his mom's house and ate more pie while Killian watched the rest of the game with his brother. It was obvious that Michael loved football. His eyes were completely animated and he actually rocked his chair a time or two in his excitement.

Seeing Michael and Killian together watching football gave me an idea for Killian's Christmas gift. It would take some planning but I was thrilled to make this gift special.

The Phoenix weather had cooled significantly and I was running each afternoon with the track team. It was only mandatory to run together twice a week, but we pushed each other. My time increased minutely, though I knew it wouldn't make much difference when the season started. I wasn't down on myself, just faced facts.

The holiday season kept me busier than usual but I loved this time of year. I spoke to Killian's mom and she agreed that I could take Michael to one of Killian's games before Christmas. I took the bus to her house several times so Michael would be comfortable around me. I loved his smile, and even with his emaciated cheekbones, every so often dimples appeared.

On game day, Michael's nurse came with us and drove the special van that transported Michael when he needed to go somewhere. I bought Michael a MacGregor jersey along with a purple and white pom-pom that he held pressed between his hands. Malory showed up early to help us get situated. I wanted to be sure Michael was in place in the skybox before the stadium went crazy with fans.

I had spoken to the team owner about my plans and everyone was in on the surprise. Michael did fantastic. He made noises when the rest of us cheered and I don't think his gentle, quirky smile left his face the entire time.

At the end of the first quarter, a picture of Michael and me hit the screen. I waved the pom-pom in Michael's hand without removing it and blew a kiss to the camera. Tears rolled down my cheeks when Killian turned from the screen, looked directly at the skybox, and blew a kiss back.

"Ah, he blew a kiss at us, Michael. Now let's hope he kicks some ass."

They did. Scorpions twenty-one, opposing team nothing.

We waited upstairs after the game to let some of the crowd clear out before taking Michael to the locker room. His nurse told me he was tired but shouldn't have a problem for another thirty minutes. We walked into the locker room and froze. All the players remained in their uniforms, minus their helmets, waiting for Michael.

"I talked to Blitz," Malory whispered.

Before I knew it, a marker was passed around, and the jersey Michael wore was signed by everyone. I watched these big, clunky, fully geared men approach slowly, talk gently to Michael, and sign his shirt.

Killian and I saw Michael off in the van, his tired eyes shutting before the vehicle pulled out.

Still in his uniform and pads, Killian pulled me close for the best make-my-lady-bits-sizzle kiss I'd had in days.

"Thank you," he said in his husky sex voice.

"Michael was wonderful," I breathed against his lips.

"So are you. Can you put up with me unwashed a little longer? I'll drop my pads, but I want to get you home."

"Hmm." I nuzzled the salty skin on his neck. "I kinda wanted to fuck you in nothing but your pads."

His throaty laugh made my head spin. "Won't work, baby. Too many clothes underneath, but we'll manage something."

"No shower," I licked his skin. "Just you and all your man sweat."

"Says the sweaty runner I love to fuck."

If he didn't get me home soon, I'd combust.

Chapter Twenty-Eight

I PUT A LOT of thought into my other Christmas gifts for Killian. A picture Malory took of us, a heavy-duty silver chain necklace with script metal work saying, "Mine," and a soft wool lap blanket for his feet when he kicked back and watched television. I knew I would use it, too, because he still liked keeping me nearly or completely naked when I cuddled up with him. It was hard to buy for Killian because he had everything, but I was very proud of my choices.

Killian bought me a brand-new silver Mustang convertible.

"But, Killian, you don't even drive a sports car," I said in stunned disbelief.

"I do now." His grin lit up his front yard.

My hands were shaking as I walked around the polished exterior. "Am I leaving it here at your house?"

"I hope not. I want you to drive it when you need it."

"Someone will steal it from my apartment." I was actually having trouble getting enough oxygen into my lungs and the words came out breathy.

He laughed, grabbed me about the waist, and swung me around in a big circle without my feet touching the ground. "Do you like it?" he asked after setting me down.

His smile was so lighthearted and he was so proud of himself. What else could I say? "I love it."

He assured me it had a tracking system and a kill switch if someone stole it.

My parents were out of town for the holiday, along with my sister, so I drove Killian to his mother's house for Christmas dinner. Beth cooked, but before dinner was ready, Killian and I took Michael to the park in the van. We walked around the small lake so he could see the ducks.

I asked Killian weeks before what Michael comprehended.

"He feels happy and sad, expresses joy and anger, but he has limited brain function."

"He loves you," I'd said.

I blinked away my thoughts about that conversation and took out the breadcrumbs I'd brought.

"Will you hold these for me, Michael?"

He smiled and moved slightly in his chair, making his wonderful happy sounds. I sat the bag on his lap and drew more than a dozen ducks our way. Things were perfect until Michael got upset when it was time to leave. I witnessed him throwing a small fit using angry sounds to mark his displeasure. I gained an entirely new perspective on the years Beth cared for Michael without help.

Killian crouched down and smoothed his palm over Michael's cheek. "We'll come back, buddy. Mom cooked a big dinner and we're hungry." Michael made angry sounds all the way home and it broke my heart.

We opened gifts after dinner. I had used all my bar jar savings to purchase Michael a life-size wall poster of Killian in uniform throwing a football. Killian hadn't known what I'd ordered and his face turned slightly red, but he helped me mount it in Michael's bedroom.

"I don't know why I didn't think of this before. It's perfect," Beth said as she admired the image of her son in his number twenty jersey.

Killian drove us home and used a slightly heavier foot on the gas pedal than I'd used on our trip to Glendale. The weather was cool, which made it one of the nicest places in the country to be on Christmas Day or evening. We drove with the top down and my cheeks were rosy and cold by the time we returned to Killian's house.

Killian had also given me a red bra and panty barely there set. I'd worn them to his mom's house with a secret smile. They didn't stay on long after we made it to bed, and I think I liked them more than the car.

Killian's last regular-season game was the week after New Year's, and they were playing Seattle. Things went from intense to a keg of dynamite waiting for someone to light a fuse. The Scorpions had only lost two games, Seattle three, if you counted the pre-season game they lost against the Scorps.

I was almost accustomed to Killian's game-day, closed-mouth habits, but this week was different. The Scorpions were going to the playoffs even if they lost, but Killian had a score to settle. Friday night, we ate at his house in bed. We never got far from it until Sunday morning. Killian was sexually insatiable. If he wasn't chafed after our sex marathon, it was never going to happen. I walked around his home on Sunday with a delicious soreness between my thighs and a satisfied smile on my face. I tried to ignore Killian's loud music blaring through the speakers.

Killian was his same silent, game-day self, but I gave him quick kisses whenever he drew close and received his burning gaze as my reward. He knew I was there and that's what mattered most.

Malory picked me up because Killian left the house even earlier than usual.

"You doing okay, sister?" she asked as soon as we took off for the stadium.

"Killian's beyond intense. How's Blitz?"

"The man needed a chill pill intravenous drip. He's psyched, and so am I. Our boys are going to the playoffs and with a little luck on their side the Super Bowl."

Amanda and Lyle joined us in the skybox. We all wore our purple jerseys waiting for kickoff. We all suffered pre-game jitters but managed to settle back in our seats when the first whistle blew.

After just two plays, a fight broke out with Killian in the thick of things. My fingers tightened on the sides of my chair, and I fought running down to the field and punching a few Seattle players myself.

Malory squeezed my arm. "Relax, Rebecca. This always happens when we play these jerks. The boys will be a little worse for wear, but they'll survive."

I took a breath and tried to enjoy the game. The Scorpions came back onto the field after halftime, up by one touchdown. The score narrowed to a three-point spread in the fourth quarter and I could barely sit still. He's going to the playoffs. He's going to the playoffs. I kept repeating it in my head because it really didn't matter what happened in this game.

Scorpions had the ball on the thirty-yard line and Killian went back in the pocket to make a pass. No one was open and I watched, in what seemed like slow motion, as he avoided a sack, turned and ran with the ball. Killian's nemesis, Blanastovich, took Killian down with a hit that lifted Killian into the air. He came down on his head at an awkward angle with his neck bent. The ball fell from his hands, but I didn't see if anyone scooped it up. Killian lay crumpled where he fell and hadn't moved since he hit the ground. From the corner of my eye, I registered that the team owner and everyone else in the skybox stood up. I stayed frozen in my seat.

This wasn't like the pre-season game. We all knew something was seriously wrong.

"Come on." Malory pulled on my hand.

I looked up.

"We need to get you down to the ambulance bay."

"No." My eyes turned back to what was taking place on the field. Killian hadn't moved at all. He wasn't conscious. Medical staff ran onto the grass.

"Rebecca, he'll be okay. You need to get down there because he will be going to the hospital."

I couldn't move.

Lyle put his arm around my shoulder and took over communication, though I had no idea what he said.

Everything was still going in slow motion. They secured Killian to a backboard, stabilizing his head and neck. I turned to Malory.

"Get me down there," I whispered.

I barely registered anything as we ran to the medical area. The head trainer was at the back of the ambulance while they loaded Killian inside. I barely got a glimpse of him. The trainer, Pete, put his arm around me while I watched the medical crew start an IV and get a heart monitor attached. I couldn't see Killian's face from where I stood because the ambulance was too high.

"He was conscious for a few minutes. He could feel his feet and legs. He's got an injury to his shoulder, but I think his neck is okay. He definitely has a concussion, but they'll tell us more at the hospital."

The words barely registered, but I understood that Killian was awake for a short time.

"I'll get her to the hospital." Malory took my hand.

Amanda hugged me, and Lyle gave me a quick kiss on the cheek.

"We'll meet you there," Lyle said as Malory pulled me away.

I prayed.

CHAPTER TWENTY-NINE

I BEGAN TREMBLING DURING the ride to the hospital. Malory turned on the heater, but it didn't help. I kept seeing Killian's lifeless body and realized I had to call his mother. I dug my cell out of my pocket and dialed. She answered immediately.

"He was conscious for a short time." I started crying.

"Are you going to the hospital?" Her voice had lost the happy inflection it usually held and I sensed her panic.

"Yes."

"I've called Michael's nurse. He's on his way, but it will be a while before I can get there. Hold onto my son, Rebecca. Don't let him go."

Hold onto Killian.

"I will."

Malory remained unnaturally calm. There was no way I could have driven at this point. We arrived at the emergency room twenty minutes after we left the stadium. Pete was waiting.

"They let me ride in the ambulance. Killian's inside. They're doing an evaluation now." Pete said all this as we walked through the doors and made our way to a private waiting room.

"Was he awake in the ambulance?" I asked.

Pete's facial muscles tightened before he answered, "No, but his vital signs were good."

"I need to see him, please."

"We'll get you in as soon as the evaluation is finished." Pete briefly squeezed my hand.

More Scorpion's organization people showed up, along with the owner. Time crawled as we all waited for some word.

As much as I didn't think I could take waiting another second, my heart froze when the doctor came out.

Pete took one of my hands and Malory the other.

"His neck and back are good. He has a broken clavicle and it's complicated. He needs surgery for realignment. The biggest problem right now is the concussion. He's in and out, but he's able to speak a few words. The CAT scan looks good, but we're delaying the surgery until he's fully conscious and we know there are no other issues." The doctor looked exhausted.

Malory stepped forward. "This is his fiancé. Can she get back there to see him?"

No one disputed her lie.

The doctor looked at me. "Yes, I can take you back, but it would be best if you come alone."

"His mother will be here shortly," I managed to say.

"Someone can escort her back when she arrives."

I followed the doctor. The room he took me into had low light and medical machines everywhere. A slow, steady beep came from the heart machine. Killian was bare from the waist up; a blanket covered his lower half. An icepack rested on his shoulder, but I could see the swelling and discoloration from the injury. I walked around and took his untethered hand. A nurse slid a chair over and I sat down.

"I'll be back to check on him shortly." The doctor left.

I couldn't take my eyes off Killian's face. I now understood why his mother didn't attend the games. I lay my head down beside Killian's and let my tears quietly soak the sheet.

I had no idea how long I stayed that way; Killian's croaky voice brought my head up.

"It's okay, baby."

He was staring at me, and without thinking, I gently kissed his lips. His eyes slowly closed and his hand squeezed mine. He grimaced and then his hand went limp again.

His mother arrived a short while later. I spoke to her outside the room first and then waited while she went inside for a private visit with her son. He didn't wake up, but the doctor said his speaking to me was a good sign because brain injuries could be tricky.

Killian was transferred to a private room on the neurological ward as a precaution a few hours later. They continued to delay the surgery, and seeing his clavicle so obviously out of joint was truly horrible.

I have no idea what time it was when Killian squeezed my hand again. I reached for his mother's hand and she joined me next to the bed. His eyelids opened and he squinted up at us.

"My head is killing me and so is my shoulder."

"You have a concussion and your clavicle needs surgery." His mother's voice was very matter of fact.

It surprised me when Killian released my hand. His went into fists, and his face screwed up in pain. I thought the pain caused his reaction, but his mother knew him better than I did.

"Killian, stop. You'll have another season, and making yourself hurt isn't helping me or Rebecca. You scared me to death and I'm not putting up with one of your tantrums right now."

My mouth dropped open. Killian didn't loosen his fists, and his mother hit the buzzer for a nurse.

"My son's awake and in pain. Could you please get him something," she said as soon as the nurse walked in.

"No," Killian ground out.

"Yes, and if you argue with me, I'll have them put the damn needle in your ass."

I had to smile over the way Beth handled her son.

Killian's fists didn't relax and the nurse placed pain medicine into his IV line. "I'll let the doctor know he's awake," she said and left us alone again.

Killian's hands opened and his eyes slowly closed. The doctor came in ten minutes later.

"We have an orthopedic surgical team standing by and we should have him in surgery in the next hour."

"Thank you, doctor. Rebecca and I need to get something to eat, but we'll be back shortly."

"I'm not hungry, Beth," I said as soon as the doctor left.

"It doesn't matter. You need to eat and so do I. I'm not arguing with you."

I followed her out of the room and down to the cafeteria. I was quickly learning where Killian got his bossiness.

Amanda and Lyle were sitting at a table, their chairs close to each other so they could see the door. They gave me a guarded look when I walked closer.

I made introductions to Killian's mother then walked over and purchased an apple and water before sitting down with my friends.

Amanda took my hand. "The entire team is in a private waiting room. Lyle and I were hoping you'd come in here eventually."

"Beth made me." I sounded like a pouty little girl and couldn't help it.

Lyle smiled and winked at Beth. "Someone needs to take her in hand."

"That's why she's perfect for my son. She's trainable and she'll be able to handle him just fine. I know these are your closest friends, Rebecca, so I'm going to speak frankly."

"Please."

Beth gave me the saddest eyes I'd ever seen from her. And though I hadn't noticed it before, they were Killian's eyes.

"I lost two boys in the cliff accident."

Chapter Thirty

I COULD DO NOTHING but listen while my heart broke all over again for Beth, Killian, and Michael.

"Killian didn't speak except to his brother that entire first year. The only reason I fought my husband so badly on turning off the machines was Killian. Michael is his twin and I couldn't separate them. I found a strength I didn't know I had. When school started, I would drop Killian off and he would just stare at me with dead eyes. He spoke to no one, not his teachers or his school friends. I picked him up each day and drove him to the hospital. Killian would walk into the room, take his brother's hand, and start talking. He'd tell him everything and then go home at night completely silent until the following day at the hospital."

Beth wiped a tear from her cheek and smiled gently.

"We found a therapist. He suggested that we keep Killian from his brother's side for two days each week and give him a chance to have time alone with his thoughts; no hospital, just a young boy who would get bored quickly. He walked more than ten miles when we tried it. A woman picked him up and gave him a ride the rest of the way to the hospital, which was forty miles away. A nurse called us. Killian had told the driver his brother was in the hospital and he needed a ride. I think it was the only words he spoke in twelve months outside of Michael's room."

Several more tears fell and I took Beth's hand.

"Eight months after the accident, Killian and Michael turned ten years old. By then, Michael had been moved to a long-term rehab facility that was closer to our home. It was a horrible birthday because Killian was determined his brother would come back to himself that day. It didn't matter what I or his therapist told him. Killian thought his brother would be okay. It was heart wrenching to see his birthday wish turn to dust.

"My husband was angry all the time and blamed himself for taking us to that summer house. He started drinking, and Killian started fighting in school. For a while, I thought

Killian got himself suspended on purpose. If he wasn't in school, he could sit with his brother."

I looked at my friends. Tears ran down Amanda's face and Lyle looked everywhere but at us. I took a drink of water not knowing how much more I could take. At the same time, I needed to hear this story.

"Angus, Killian's father, left about a year after the accident. It was almost a blessing. I went back to work part-time to help make ends meet. Slowly, Killian started talking again, but he wasn't the same child I'd known for nine years. He still spoke to Michael and I heard him say he would make enough money when he was older so Michael could live back at home. His fights at school didn't stop. I had to transfer him twice. Angus lost his job and with it his health insurance. I had to move Michael into a lower-priced facility and I rented a home close by in a poorer section of town. There was nothing else I could do. I have no idea how many busted noses and split lips I doctored on Killian. Those were the wounds I could see.

"It shocked the hell out of me when Killian told me he was trying out for the high school freshman football team. Somewhere in Killian's mind, he'd decided he could learn to play football and go pro to pay for all the things we needed. The fights slowed down and you never saw Killian anywhere without a football in his hand. We'd visit Michael and Killian would rest that ball in Michael's lap. 'He smiled mom,' he said the first time Michael reacted. And it was amazing because it was true. After that, if Killian wasn't in school or at the rehabilitation center, he practiced. The varsity coach took notice and Killian was the starting quarterback his junior year. He took all his pent-up rage and put it into the game. He's never stopped."

Beth squeezed my hand and continued. "Angus died in an automobile accident Killian's first year of college. He wasn't drunk, but a drunk driver hit and killed him. We'd never filed for divorce, so I received the insurance settlement. Killian and I made the decision together that I would quit my job and bring Michael home. I never saw Killian's college games, but when he wasn't in class or at practice, he spent every spare second helping me care for Michael. Killian even let me go on a few dates while he stayed with his brother. The Scorpions drafted Killian in the first round. He didn't buy anything for himself for two years, but he moved us here, bought my house, and paid for nurses to help care for Michael."

Beth turned in her chair and took both my hands. "Since meeting you, he's slowly come back to me. He's happy outside of football and I never thought I would see that. Two years ago, Killian promised his brother he'd win the Super Bowl for him. Killian isn't going to take this well. Have patience with him, and whatever you do, don't let go."

What could I do or say? This woman had been through so much and loved her boys. I loved them, too.

"I won't. I promise."

Killian's surgery took two hours and he came through without complications. I went down and spoke with his teammates and then Amanda drove me to my apartment to shower and change clothes. I hurried back to the hospital so Beth could get home to Michael and be sure he was okay.

I walked back into Killian's room. He was awake and staring straight up at the ceiling. I tried speaking to him, but he refused to acknowledge I was there. I thought about everything Beth told me and realized Killian had to be the most stubborn man on the planet. I could play that game, too, so I refused to leave. His silence was heartbreaking, but not as bad as when one of his teammates showed up. Killian gave me a dead look, and, using monosyllable words, told me to step out of the room. This went on for two days. I arrived at the hospital to take him home on the third day. Blitz was in the room packing Killian's things.

"Can you give me a minute, Blitz?" Killian asked him.

Blitz left the room and Killian looked at me for a long minute before speaking. "I'm fine, Rebecca. It would be better if you went back to your apartment. I won't be needing your help."

My heart clenched and my stomach tightened in misery. "Don't do this, Killian. You do need help and that's what people do when they love each other."

His gaze never left mine. "Then maybe that's the problem. I don't love you enough and I don't want you caring for me."

I stared for a moment and then straightened my back and challenged him. "You're a fool." Anger tightened every muscle in my body.

"If it makes you feel better, you can give me a going home blow job. Otherwise, it's time that you leave."

He did not just say that!

I took several deep breaths and walked toward him. He very calmly pulled back the sheet and lifted his hospital gown. He was going from semi-erect to a full erection. I wanted to grab his dick and twist. Hard. Looking into his eyes, I saw no emotion. I turned and walked out the door.

Fuck Killian MacGregor.

Chapter Thirty-One

I DIDN'T RUN FOR two days. On the third, I angrily pulled on my running clothes and ran until I almost passed out. I pushed again the following morning. It became my daily stress reliever.

A week after leaving the hospital, I called Killian's mother.

"I tried." I could barely speak because of the sobs built up in my throat.

"I know, dear. Don't cry. Killian will snap out of it. He's stubborn and doesn't want anyone around right now." Weariness was evident in each word Beth spoke.

"Have you seen him?"

"Yes, last night. It wasn't pleasant. If not for his injury, I'd take a two-by-four to his head."

The thought of Killian in pain made me cringe, but her words also helped me gain control of my emotions. "Is someone helping him?"

"Not really. Killian works through these things in his own way and eventually he'll come to terms that he isn't infallible. Shit happens and it's not the end of the world."

I needed to change the subject. Thinking of Killian alone in his large home, in pain, with no one helping him hurt deeply. "How's Michael?"

"He's aware things are tense right now. You visiting might calm him."

"I would love to."

"Are you available tomorrow night at six?"

"Perfect. What can I bring?"

After we ended our conversation, I called Amanda.

"Can you follow me to Killian's so I can drop the Mustang off tomorrow night?"

"Give it more time, Rebecca. The jerk will come around sooner or later."

Amanda called Killian "the jerk" every chance she got. I understood and knew she cared about me, but I loved Killian.

"Amanda," I chided.

"I know, but he is a jerk."

"Will you help me tomorrow night or not?"

"Of course I'll help you."

Killian had his own key to the Mustang. I used the remote on the visor and opened the large wrought iron gate at Killian's house. I locked the key inside the car along with a brief note. Amanda drove me to Beth's and dropped me off.

Seeing Beth and Michael was wonderful and also heartbreaking. We ate dinner, talked about anything non-Killian and took Michael for a walk after wrapping him tightly in blankets.

"Thank you for having me over, Beth."

"You're welcome and you're invited any time."

Over Beth's objections, I took the bus home. I had to walk half a mile from the bus stop to my apartment, but it felt good, even in the chilly air.

I turned the last corner and saw the Mustang parked on the street. A thrill went through me. It lasted until I saw the note on my door.

Rebecca,

The car is a gift and I'm NOT returning the gifts you gave to me. I've packed your personal items from my house and secured them in the trunk. This is for the best and eventually, if you haven't already, you will understand I am no good for you.

K

Anger squeezed my heart. He was walking away because he fucking got hurt. He wasn't going to the Super Bowl, so he no longer needed me.

I found both keys to the Mustang under the front mat. I removed the items from the trunk, mostly clothes, and walked them to the nearest Dumpster. If Killian was present I would have shredded every last piece in front of him. I managed to control myself and not kick the Mustang.

I put the keys in a drawer and decided to forget the car belonged to me, because in my mind, it didn't.

After I crawled into bed, my anger turned to tears. Killian punished himself by getting rid of me. The thought just made me cry harder.

I hit the pavement the following morning and increased my time by five minutes. Track was starting soon and it was my last year. I decided to give it everything I had. Over the following weeks, I immersed myself in running and academics.

"Eight minutes under your best time, Cavanaugh," my couch shouted.

I'd cut my morning run to ten miles because Monday through Friday I was running with the team each afternoon. Our first meet was three weeks away and it was one month post-Killian. Running exorcised my demons, so I gave it everything I had.

The Scorpions had lost the first game of the playoffs the week after Killian was injured. I felt bad for the entire team and had spoken to Malory once over the phone.

"Blitz is impossible to live with. You'd think they announced the end of the world. The guys had a drink fest at Killian's this past weekend and I left early." She stopped talking for a moment. "I'm sorry, Rebecca. I shouldn't mention Killian, but I have no idea what's come over the man."

I kept my tone light, though I felt sick to my stomach. "No, you shouldn't mention Killian, but I feel bad for the entire team."

"Yeh, so do I. We need to get together and drown our sorrows," she said half-heartedly.

"I'm in season right now and not drinking. Maybe after I graduate we can get together."

Our phone call ended painfully. Things weren't the same, and I was no longer the girlfriend. I really didn't belong in Malory's world and I knew it.

My first meet approached and I rested two days prior, giving my body a break. I'd lost weight I couldn't afford to lose, but other than a broken heart, I felt in the best shape of my life. Amanda and Lyle took me out to dinner Thursday night and, unfortunately, we ran into my sister.

"Hi, sis. I heard the quarterback dumped you," Candi said with pure malice.

Thankfully, Amanda and I occupied a booth and Amanda had the inside seat. I pushed against her when I thought she might fly over me and across the table at my sister. The two of them had never gotten along.

"Yes, Candi, I got dumped. Is there anything else you need?"

Candi's face twisted into a sneer. "I saw Killian's brother at that game. I bet you were so happy with yourself."

"Why would I be happy with myself?"

"You thought I might sink low enough to go out with some idiot with money."

This time, Lyle and Amanda held me back while my sister just stood there looking bored.

"Michael MacGregor is entirely too good for you, but if you play your cards right, Killian is available and the two of you deserve each other. I'd keep your comments to myself, though, because Killian loves Michael."

"You're pathetic, sis. Like I'd take a chance one of my kids would get that gene."

Amanda dropped my arm. "Lyle let her go. Kick her ass, Rebecca. She's needed it for years. I don't normally believe in violence, but I'm changing my opinion."

I looked at my friends and they looked back at me. Lyle broke first and then we all started laughing. It felt good and by the look on Candi's face, it had the desired effect. She left.

"Are you sure the two of you are related?" Lyle asked.

"I've thought for years that I was adopted. I'm so much taller than my mom, look nothing like Candi, and usually don't have her bitchy disposition. Maybe she was dropped on her head at birth."

Amanda picked up her water glass and proposed a toast. "Here's to bitchy sisters, fucked up straight men, and friendship."

We clinked our glasses. "Here, here."

I loved my friends and when all was said and done, I loved my sister. I also felt sorry for her. I didn't think she'd ever truly known love from a man. Though my heart still hurt with Killian's loss, I wouldn't change anything but the ending of our relationship.

And I was afraid I would always love Killian MacGregor.

Chapter Thirty-Two

I WOKE UP SATURDAY morning with far more excitement than I'd felt in weeks. I'd been pushing myself harder than ever before. Middle-of-the-pack Cavanaugh was ready to move up a place or two. It felt good to know I had a shot of doing exactly that. It was a four-school track meet and I wanted to know if my preparations paid off.

The starting pistol sounded and the 10,000-meter race began. Within twenty steps I picked an inside line and held my ground. I established my place in the pack and stuck to it. My leg muscles were loose with my fingers lightly touching my palms. I looked ahead, focusing on my goal. I sank into my rhythm quicker than I'd ever done before and let the outside world drift away.

At the halfway point, there were two distinct groups. I stayed slightly to the rear of the front one. More runners fell back as the race continued. Eventually, I felt the strain in my legs, but also their power. When the flag signaling the final four laps went up, I usually felt the wear and tear on my body, but not this time. I moved up a few runners and quickly counted six in front of me. I held my ground as the pace picked up slightly. Three laps, two laps, I was now in fourth position. I rounded the turn to begin my last lap. My legs, with a will of their own, kicked it into high gear. My fucking long legs, that I always hated, ate up the synthetic rubber track beneath my shoes. I made the last curve and gave an additional burst of speed.

I, Rebecca Lesley Cavanaugh, won my first college race.

The closest runner finished two seconds behind me. I accepted congratulations from other runners as we walked our cool down. I waved into the stands. My parents waited at the field exit and hugged my tall, sweaty body.

"We're so proud of you," my father said.

I gave them both a kiss and turned to find Amanda literally jumping up and down with excitement. Lyle stood beside her with a huge smile plastered on his face. I hugged them both and looked up and past them to a semi-crowd about forty yards away.

It was Killian surrounded by college fans. I don't think he saw me as he extricated himself from admirers and walked the opposite direction from where I stood.

"I need to get showered and then let's celebrate." My voice somehow remained steady.

Amanda and Lyle agreed, but my parents begged off. Lyle and Amanda said they'd wait for me. I stood under the spray of the shower and fought tears.

Why the hell did Killian come to my meet? I'd shed so many tears for him, but this was my day, my win, my success. I didn't want him anywhere near me. I needed to move on with my life and find happiness without him.

At that moment, I wanted to fucking wring Killian Mac-Gregor's neck.

❧❧❧❧❧ ❧❧❧❧❧

The bar was packed with college students, mostly athletes. I usually stayed away from the after-meet hangout, but Lyle and Amanda wanted me to have the full benefit of my win. I also decided to cheat this one night on my season anti-inebriety rule. Rebecca, the boring sister, tied one on.

"I think you've had your fair share of alcohol and we need to be leaving," Lyle said.

"Yep, come on. Let's get you tucked into bed, Rebecca," Amanda added.

"Nope, you guys go on without me. I'm having fun."

I'd danced with a tall, medium-distance runner, and was now sweaty and waiting for another drink to cool me off. My head spun, but I felt wonderful. I briefly wondered what I would do if a guy's dick slipped into my face tonight. I stumbled slightly and Lyle steadied me.

"We aren't going anywhere without you, Rebecca. You're stuck with us."

I giggled and threw my arms around him.

"You're my bestest boyfriend." I pulled Amanda into my hug, too. "And you're my bestest girlfriend."

Amanda hugged me back and said, "You are going to pay for this tomorrow."

"Killian came to my meet today. Why do you think he did that?"

"Oh, honey." Amanda sighed.

"Don't. I'm not crying over that football turd again. He just needs to leave me alone."

"Come on."

Lyle pulled slightly on my arm, but I jerked away.

"No, I'm going to look for a dick. You two go home."

The room continued spinning, but I didn't care. I saw my dancing partner and made my way to him.

"Wanna dance?" I asked.

This was the new me. Rebecca Cavanaugh, the winner.

"I got a better idea. Let's get out of here."

"I wanna dance first," I pouted.

"Whatever the lady wants, but then I know a nice place you can relax and we can get to know each other a little better."

"You're on Mr. Tall Runner. I like a man I can look up to."

He took me to the dance floor and spun me around, making my head whirl even more. The music changed and he brought me in close; his hand went to my ass and I imagined it was Killian's. In my drunkenness, I also imagined his voice.

"That's enough. Get your hands off her."

My tall runner stopped dancing. I turned slightly and saw Killian. He didn't look happy. I take that back. He looked furious.

The hands holding me disappeared and so did my dance partner.

"Why the hell did you do that?" I yelled above the music.

"Because your friend called and told me to come and fix my problem."

"What problem?" I stumbled and Killian grabbed my arms.

"You, Rebecca. You're my problem."

I wrenched away. "I wanna dance and not with you. Go home with my friends. I'm gonna find someone taller than you to dance with."

"Let's go." Killian grabbed my hand and started toward the door.

"No," I shouted and pulled away.

The dancing stopped and people stared, but I didn't care. How dare Killian rain on my happy parade?

I looked around for help. Before I knew what happened, Killian swung me up and over his shoulder.

"Put me down," I screamed, but all I heard was laughter. I stopped thinking about everything else because all of a sudden I knew I was going to hurl all over Killian's backside.

"I'm getting sick."

I didn't realize we were outside when Killian sat me quickly on my feet. I turned away and vomited. He tried to pull my hair from my face, but even as sick as I was, I didn't want him touching me.

"Go away," I said between heaves while pushing at his hands.

"I'm not going anywhere until you're home and tucked into bed, Rebecca. Stop fighting me."

"No."

My liquor and bar food spewed to the ground. When my stomach finished heaving, I stood and tried to walk back into the bar. Killian grabbed my hand tightly, pulling me around to the other side of his car.

I went into petulance mode and crossed my arms as he tried to get the chest strap across my body. Killian jerked my arms down and buckled me in.

"If you remove the seat belt I will spank your ass."

"I hate you," I mumbled in absolute misery. My poor head wouldn't stop spinning.

Halfway to my apartment, Killian needed to pull over again. He didn't try to touch me this time, just waited patiently, buckled me back inside, and finished the drive to my apartment. I came to briefly when Killian carried me inside.

I didn't remember much after that.

Chapter Thirty-Three

I GROANED AND PULLED the pillow over my head. My head hurt, my body hurt, but worst of all, my pride was shattered.

I was afraid to open my eyes and find Killian in my apartment. I didn't hear noise but continued to assess my surroundings for several more minutes. I finally removed the pillow and squinted into the daylight with one eye.

My poor, pathetic head.

My mouth tasted horrible and I thought I might be sick again. I scooted my legs around and slowly went to a sitting position.

Two pills, a glass of water, and a note rested on the bedside table.

Legs,

Take the ibuprofen, shower, and eat something. Get some rest today. I'm picking you up for dinner at six.

K

Over my dead body.

Killian MacGregor was not prancing back into my life.

My head pounded dully, so I took the pills because I didn't really have a choice. I also spent an hour in the shower, which pissed me off more because it was exactly what the note told me to do. I managed to eat a piece of toast before falling back into bed. I slept for a few more hours and felt half-human when I woke up. I took another shower, though this one shorter, dressed quickly, and with an overnight bag hung across my arm, left my apartment.

Fuck Killian MacGregor.

Amanda let me in.

"If you call that son of a bitch, I'll never speak to you again," were the first words out of my mouth.

"It was Lyle who called him last night, so keep your panties on."

"Lyle is off the best friend list for at least a week. I'm staying the night."

"I'll order pizza."

My stomach rumbled unhappily. "I'll watch you eat it."

Amanda laughed. "You really tied one on last night, girl-friend."

"I'm never drinking again."

·"Probably a wise move."

We watched all the old Jason Bourne movies and lusted over Matt Damon. Movie boyfriends and book boyfriends were the way I planned to go for the rest of my life.

My phone rang at seven, but I ignored it. Before we went to bed, Amanda sat with me while I put Killian's message on speakerphone.

"Hiding won't work, Legs. We need to talk."

Short, sweet, and to the point.

Too damn bad!

"Do you plan on calling him?" Amanda asked carefully.

"No."

"You know you love him, right?" She gave me her sad face.

"I know, but I can't go through that again. I'll get over him eventually." I lied to Amanda and myself.

I tossed and turned the entire night. Amanda dropped me at my apartment early so I could get my morning run in. I hadn't packed my gear or I would have run to my apartment. I put on my shoes, tied the laces, and did a few stretches. Closing the front door behind me, I turned and ran directly into Killian's chest.

His arms came up and he brought me in close. He felt so fucking good, but I pulled back.

"No, Killian. I'm not speaking to you. I'm not listening to you and I'm not going anywhere with you."

He released my arms. I turned and set off at a faster pace than normal. I heard Killian's shoes hit the pavement behind me. He was dressed in running clothes. I ignored him or at least tried. He made it to the same soccer field he had the first time before his steps faded into the distance.

I went to class and then practice. My coach took me aside.

"You know you've always been capable of winning, Cavanaugh."

"Well, maybe."

"No, completely capable."

What could I say?

"I plan to work you harder than you've ever worked. You're in a position to help this team and we need seniors to stand up and take the lead. You did that at the meet."

"Thank you, sir." I walked back over to my teammates.

The next morning, Killian was waiting outside my door again.

I ignored him.

It pissed me off that he was ruining my peaceful morning runs, but I refused to acknowledge him in any way, even if it was only to tell him how I felt. He made it farther, but I still left him in my dust.

Wednesday morning, the same thing. I was leaving the following day for an out-of-state meet. I was determined to make it silently through my run.

"How long are you going to keep this up, Legs?"

I stopped and turned. "Stop calling me that, stop following me, and please just get out of my life." I turned and started running again.

"No."

Killian made it an entire extra mile before he stopped.

I thought he might show up that night at Tillomans, but to my relief, he stayed away. I didn't run the following morning because of the road trip and couldn't help wondering if Killian waited for me to come outside. I left my apartment at ten in the morning and felt a sense of relief when the bus pulled away. Killian had me on edge and I needed to relax.

The meet was only between two teams, and the other college was smaller than ours. I'd placed fourth against them the year before and thought I had a decent chance of performing well this time. Fourth was my best run last season.

I was wrong. I didn't place well; I won. My long legs had finally decided to do me proud. It was a heady feeling and would have been perfect, but Killian stood outside the visiting locker room when I walked out, a few of my teammates by my side. Their eyes got huge when they looked from Killian to me.

"This is stalking."

Killian showed his killer dimples, but I wasn't impressed. He had no shame.

"This is love."

The ladies around me giggled and I wanted to groan and kick his nuts.

"Go away, Killian." I turned and walked away.

"Never, Rebecca."

I flounced onto the bus. We were staying in a hotel not far away and heading back to Phoenix the following morning.

"Did you just turn down Killian MacGregor?" one of my teammates asked.

"Yes, and it's not the first time."

"Is he really stalking you?" another asked.

"Yes, and it's not the first time."

More giggles released inside the bus.

The team left me alone after that. Unfortunately, I wanted to do nothing more than cry. My roommate went out for dinner and I begged off. I ordered a light meal from room service and flipped through channels until a soft knock sounded at the door.

I didn't bother looking out the peephole, which was terribly stupid because Killian walked inside as soon as the door opened.

"Don't do this, Killian, please, I—"

That was as far as I got. Killian's lips slammed into mine. He wasn't gentle. My breathing accelerated within seconds. His mouth, the taste of him, his tongue. I was home and the deep ache I'd carried with me for more than a month disappeared. His hands went to my breasts and I groaned into his mouth. He pulled my bra and shirt over my head. My pants fell to my feet within seconds. Killian lifted me up and I wrapped my legs around his hips. He hadn't done more than unzip himself, but his cock was untethered and poised to enter. He looked at me and slowly slid inside.

God, I missed this. I missed him. Killian and all his fucked-up ideals about winning.

He fucked me against the door. I didn't think about the bruises he would leave on my hips or the large hole in my heart. The steady in-and-out slide of his cock was my entire world. And his eyes. Their intensity pierced me as deeply as his dick slid inside me.

My body clenched and that overwhelming achy feeling of need refused to settle. It built—deep, mind-blowing heat. I couldn't hold back any longer. I dug my nails into his back, through his shirt, wanting to feel his flesh tear. I tried to kiss him, but he refused to stop watching me. My head tipped back and I screamed.

When I finally took in my surroundings, I was on the floor sitting in Killian's lap. He ran his fingers through my hair and all my pent-up emotions released. I started crying.

"Shh, baby. I'm sorry. You don't deserve an asshole like me, but I can't stay away. I love you."

I clenched his shirt into my fingers and balled my eyes out.

Finally, Killian moved me off his lap and stood, pulling me up beside him. He settled me into bed.

A knock sounded on the door.

"That's my dinner."

"Good, you need to eat."

Killian opened the door, took the tray, and brought it back to the bed.

"Where's your roommate?"

"She went out to dinner and then probably to a nightclub. You shouldn't be here; it's against school rules."

"I like breaking rules." He smiled so tenderly I almost started crying again. "But I'll leave as soon as you eat. You've lost weight and I don't like seeing you like this."

Killian removed the cover of the two dishes and smiled. I'd ordered the largest hamburger they had, which came with French-fries, and I added a side order of fries. I needed my calories after the race.

He sat on the side of the bed and watched me eat the burger.

"Have some fries," I mumbled through my food. I was hungrier than I'd been since Killian dumped me.

He took a few bites but soon started feeding me. He'd roll a fry in ketchup, just the way I liked, and put it to my lips.

"I've missed you, Rebecca."

"I've missed you, too, Killian."

He didn't say anything after that. When the last fry was gone, he wiped my lips with a napkin, kissed me tenderly but quickly, and walked out of the room carrying my tray. I rolled over to my side and wondered what the hell I was going to do. I didn't have enough willpower to resist him and didn't think any woman could. If there was an anti-boyfriend pill, I'd spend all my bar jar money to buy one. Killian would break my heart again and I didn't think I could survive.

Someone needed to put me out of my misery.

Chapter Thirty-Four

Monday morning Killian waited out front and followed me when I took off running. He didn't say anything, just kept pace. It was chilly and looked like rain was heading in.

He stopped at the five-mile mark, slightly shorter than the distance he normally ran, and went back the way he came. I continued, and finished my run before the rain began.

Killian waited at my door.

I looked at him. "Nothing's changed, Killian. This won't work."

I watched him close his eyes for a moment before opening them and giving me the smallest hint of dimples.

"I won't give up, Rebecca, though I know I deserve everything you're putting me through."

My rage kicked in. "You have no idea what you've put me through. How many tears I've cried or how many times I'd give anything to be in your arms one last time. I'm broken, Killian. You broke me. I don't want the pain that goes along with being your girlfriend."

He leaned in and kissed me. No tongue, just a short, sweet kiss with barely parted lips.

"I love you," he said, but he didn't kiss me again. He turned and walked away.

Killian wasn't waiting for me the following morning and my heart dropped into my belly. It was hard, but I stuck with my normal course. Everything I saw reminded me of Killian. I ran on the path and looked down for a minute at some fallen branches in my way before looking back up. I entered the soccer field park. Killian, with Michael bundled up warmly in his wheelchair, waited for me. As I ran closer, I made out a sign resting against Michael's chest.

"I love you and my brother does, too," was written in bold black letters.

I could have killed Killian. I slowed a few feet from Michael, and bent and kissed his cheek, gently squeezing his hands.

"I've missed you, Michael, but your brother is a rascal for pulling you into this."

Michael made his pleased noises that I loved to hear.

I released him, rose to my full height, and gave Killian my best "You are a dick" glare.

He wasn't intimidated.

I finished my run.

The following morning, the sign read, "If she's a screamer, she's a keeper."

I gave Michael the same kiss as the day before and didn't even bother glaring at Killian. The man had no shame.

Killian and his mother came to Tillomans during my shift that evening. I hadn't seen Beth in more than a month and it felt good to have her arms circle around me.

"You're doing wonderful, dear. Don't make this easy on him," she whispered in my ear.

I wiped a tear away and turned to Killian. "Do you know what you'd like, sir?"

His eyes sparkled with merriment. "Yes, you."

The jerk. He'd said it in front of his mother. Beth laughed. I wished I had a tray of food, because I would have dumped it in his lap.

"I'll take tonight's special," Beth said into the blaring silence.

"If I can't have you, I'll have the same."

"That's enough, Killian. She's at work."

"Yes, Mother."

I stormed off, hoping I could find another server to take my place. No one was willing. They knew about my past with Killian and obviously wanted to see the fireworks.

Surprisingly, he behaved himself throughout the rest of his meal.

The sign in Michael's arms the following morning read, "Long legs make me pant."

I don't know what Killian said to his brother, but he was making all kinds of noises when I got close enough to hear. This was a new low and I so wanted to box Killian's ears.

"Good morning, Michael. I love you, but your brother is a good-for-nothing dog." I kept my voice completely sweet. Killian let out a low-sounding dog growl.

I left Michael and his deviant brother standing there while I finished my run. I really couldn't take much more of this. My heart was melting and I was at the breaking point.

Friday the sign said, "Can my brother pick you up tonight for a sleepover?"

It was only six in the morning, but other people ran or walked at this time of day. I wondered what they thought. They had to recognize Killian, but obviously he didn't care.

I kissed Michael. "Yes, I'll be waiting."

What the hell was I doing? I was a fool, but Killian was so far under my skin that I couldn't help myself.

Killian arrived promptly at five.

"Grab the Mustang keys, Legs."

"Why?" I looked at him suspiciously.

"Because I know you haven't used it and it needs to be driven."

I placed the keys in his palm. "You can keep the car, Killian."

"No, I cannot."

He pulled me into his body and kissed me. His teeth tugged on my bottom lip until I opened my mouth and his tongue swooped in. My lady bits tingled and my heart raced. Pulling back, Killian placed his fingers on my cheeks and tilted my head back so I stared into his eyes.

"I'm so sorry, Rebecca, and I don't deserve you, but I love you. We'll talk at my place."

"I'd rather just fuck." It was mean and bitchy, but I couldn't help myself.

His lips quirked and one dimple appeared. "We'll do that, too."

He released my face and took my hand. Even though the promise of fucking Killian made my insides sizzle, it was actually his hand holding mine that I missed the most. His touch. Such a simple thing, but so powerful. I wiped a few tears from my eyes.

After situating me in the car and taking the driver's seat, Killian didn't release my hand. I closed my eyes and let myself absorb his thumb running across my fingers. My body craved Killian's touch and the hole in my heart grew smaller.

Killian hopelessly outmaneuvered me.

Chapter Thirty-Five

His home was exactly as I remembered. I tried to harden my heart, but when he led me immediately into his bedroom, his unique scent lingering in the air turned my belly to quivering jelly. Within a few seconds, panic set in. I put my hands out in front of me after he placed my bag on the floor.

"I'm sorry. I don't think I can do this. It hurts too much, Killian."

He didn't move closer. "Talk to me, love."

My voice rose slightly. "How can I? I shouldn't have come. I really can't handle you or your need to win. I'm not cut out to be part of your life."

He spoke so softly. "I've changed."

A burst of deriding laughter slipped past my lips. "No, you haven't, Killian. Winning to you is all-inclusive. You call it focus and I call it insanity. You play a game and the 'powers that be' pay you a lot of money. I get that. But, when it's all said and done, it's a game. Boys out on a field, pounding each other into the mud. A game."

Killian's eyes went dark. "It's more than a game, Rebecca."

Why had I come here and put myself through this? Yes, I was horny and lonely, but most of all weak. "It's a game."

His fingers ran through his hair and he turned away.

I managed to take a slow, calming breath. I could do this.

"Sit down, please," he said when he turned back.

"In here?"

"Yes, in here."

"You know you can temporarily change my mind with sex. You've done it before, but a relationship is more than sex. It's caring for each other at our weakest moments, holding the other tight when we're sad or in your case devastated. You shut me out, destroyed me. When you needed me most you fucking threw me away. No, Killian, I won't have this conversation here in your fuck room."

I walked out and realized I'd said everything I could say. I headed to the front door.

Killian grabbed my hand.

"I can walk away from football, Rebecca, but I can't let you walk away from me."

My broken heart ripped a little further.

"I'm sorry I came here today. I know you're hurting and I really don't want you to suffer any more. I want to stop suffering, too."

"Then stay with me." His voice was ragged.

I was such a complete and utter fool and so tired of fighting my needs. "Just fuck me, Killian. Make my body tingle and give me orgasms that rock my world. I really miss fucking you."

For just a moment, and based on the look on his face, I didn't think he would take me up on my offer. I turned to the door, but one of Killian's hands went into my hair while the other pulled me back by my arm.

He was angry, but so was I. He ripped my shirt and I made sure he'd have furrows on his arms and back for a week to come. We ended up with me on my hands and knees, on the floor, on top of our clothing. He practically pulled my hair out by the roots as he held me in place. His other arm braced beneath my stomach after he roughly spread my legs wider.

I was wet, but the sudden force of his cock driving into me hurt. His fullness pushed inside me until he could go no farther. My fingers sank into the clothes beneath my hands. He pulled out and slammed back in. The cries coming from my throat begged him for more.

"Fuck me, Killian. Don't stop."

He didn't say a word, just kept pounding in and out.

There was nothing loving about our coupling. Killian MacGregor fucked me just like I asked. Every nerve ending I had led to my pussy. The ache didn't build slowly, it exploded outward, over much too fast. I screamed, but Killian wasn't through with me. The sting of his teeth in my shoulder caused pressure to build again. He used his cock without mercy. I don't know if my first orgasm ever stopped. Killian's cry was a loud animal sound and his teeth found another spot. He pulled back, bringing me with him so I was sitting with my back to his chest, his cock buried deep.

"I'll fuck you all weekend if that's all you'll take from me, Rebecca." His hot breath blew into my ear.

"Yes." I gave another low moan.

He slipped from my body, stood and picked me up. With purposeful strides, he carried me into the bedroom where he tossed me on the bed. Unbelievably, his cock was hard and I couldn't help staring.

Killian followed the direction of my eyes and smiled. "This is what you do to me. I'm going to fuck you again, but slower this time."

"Slow's not fucking," I choked out.

"You won't have any doubt that's what it is when I'm through. Spread your legs."

"Killian."

"Spread your fucking legs, Rebecca. If this is all I can have then I'm taking every last bit you'll give me."

The burn between my thighs was back and it wasn't caused by the rough sex we'd just had. I lay back and spread my legs.

His finger went to my pussy and he moved far enough up my body so he could comfortably suck my nipples. He started with slow, shallow strokes of his finger while he licked and pinched my breasts. When he pinched particularly hard, his finger went in farther before slowly pulling out. The delicious pain traveled my entire body, curling my toes..

"Please, Killian," I begged without shame, my pelvis lifting to meet his palm.

"I could do this for hours and keep you right on the edge."

"No." I groaned and opened my eyes.

Killian glanced at me, my nipple between his lips. He pulled his lips back so his teeth held my skin. He applied biting pressure and added another finger until I cried out. The rhythm between my legs slowed and his tongue twirled delicately around my areola. He moved his head to my other breast and started again. I bucked my hips and sank my hands into his hair.

"I can't take any more, Killian." I couldn't get enough air and felt light-headed.

He moved on top of me and slid his cock slowly inside. I still had my fingers in his hair and pulled him to my lips. He kept a slow, steady thrust between my legs and mimicked the movement of his tongue with his cock.

I needed hard again, but he wouldn't go faster. My orgasm stayed right on the brink; I wanted more pelvic pressure and a faster glide, but Killian refused. I had no idea where he got his stamina. My entire body quivered. Finally, the orgasm rolled over me in one endless wave and I cried out my release. As the last ripples faded, Killian shoved into me hard and held his body still.

"All day and all night, Rebecca. I'll make you scream each and every time."

If she's a screamer, she's a keeper. I remembered the sign.

Killian was turning me into a keeper.

Chapter Thirty-Six

He washed me thoroughly in the shower. I tried to do it myself, but he removed the soap from my hands and cleaned every inch of my skin.

"You're punishing me." Sadness tinged my voice.

Momentarily, his soapy hands stopped moving. "No, I'm giving you what you asked for."

"Then you're punishing yourself."

His gaze darkened. "But will it be enough, Rebecca? Can you forgive me? Will you love me again?"

I pulled him into my arms. I could see the pain in his eyes and I was so afraid to tell him how much I loved him. I never stopped and didn't think I ever would. It was me. I was punishing both of us, but I couldn't stop. The weeks and months of pain made me into a person I didn't know. I wanted to wipe it all away, let my heart melt again, and most of all forgive him.

Why was I doing this?

My tears started and my shoulders began shaking.

"Shh, Rebecca, it's okay. I understand. I'll do whatever it takes. I'm not going anywhere and if I eventually get my way, you'll never go anywhere again. Please let me know when I can stop fucking you."

"Never," I cried.

"Okay," he whispered.

"But love me, too, Killian. I can't stop."

"Never stop baby."

He rinsed me off, wrapped me in a towel, and instead of carrying me to bed, he carried me to the kitchen and rested my butt on the same barstool I occupied that first night.

"You've lost weight and need to eat."

"What are we having?"

"I have no idea, but I'm sure it's good."

Killian's waist was wrapped in a towel that separated on the side of his hip, giving me a glimpse of naked flesh. We were back to naked games and I smiled. He turned and his grin answered mine.

"You're beautiful." His dimples grew.

"You're sexy." My smile widened.

"Stop that. Eating, then lovemaking. In that order."

"Okay."

We ate lasagna and drank red wine. It was the first alcohol I'd had since getting drunk after my I won the meet. I needed it tonight, not a lot, but enough to take the edge off my nerves.

I finished my last bite, feeling Killian's eyes on me. "Talk to me, please," I whispered.

"Where do you want to talk?"

"On the couch."

"Come on." He helped me from my chair and didn't let go of my hand as he led me to the couch.

After we sat down, I reluctantly pulled my fingers away. Killian watched me clasp my hands and place them in my lap. He took a deep breath, but didn't speak.

I took the lead. "What changed your mind?"

"I never changed my mind, because I never stopped loving you."

I almost got up, but I could see he wanted to continue.

"I couldn't see past my injury, my dream, or the promise to my brother. Football has been my life since I decided it would give me the things Michael and my mom needed.

You moved everything around. That wasn't a bad thing. I thought I could have it all, but 'all' for me is winning."

Now his eyes turned away and my fingernails dug into my skin.

"My mother had a few things to say and she set me straight." He took a very deep breath and let it out. His gaze settled back on mine. "It doesn't matter what I do, Michael will never come back. He doesn't care if I win or lose a game. He only cares that I talk to him and spend time with him. He gets as much enjoyment, maybe more, from seeing the ducks as he does watching a football game. I'm an adult, but there was still a small piece of my nine-year-old self that had a spark of hope. If I won, he would come back."

Tears welled in Killian's eyes and slid down his face. "I found him in the river, touched him, but then let go and came up for air. Thirty, forty-five seconds may have made a difference. I let him go. My twin brother who I loved so much. He wouldn't have let me go."

I couldn't help it; my own tears were falling. I launched myself at Killian. He had no choice but to grab me, but he kept talking.

"My mother laid things out for me. Michael will never be the Michael I had. Nothing I do will change that. But, the

Michael I had would have wanted me happy. Football and winning," Killian paused and moved me back so we were looking into each other's eyes. "don't make me happy. You do. I'm nothing without you. The game means nothing, my life means nothing. I love you more than I love Michael."

I spoke through my tears. "No, Killian, you don't. Love stretches and accommodates new love. There's no limits."

He pulled me in close. "You're so wrong. We will lose Michael someday. His health is iffy at best. He doesn't have enough resistance to illness. It's a miracle we've had so many good years. When he's gone, I'll go on, but, Rebecca, I won't go on without you." He shuddered against me.

"I love you so much." I barely got the words out. "I'm so sorry for what I've put you through."

That laughing rumble in his chest felt so good. "You aren't nearly as sorry as I am. I was so stupid, so incredibly selfish. I love you more than life itself."

"Will you make love to me now?"

The rumble came again. "I've never just fucked you, Rebecca. Every sigh, every shiver that runs across your flesh settles in my heart. I can love you hard or soft, but it's love. Don't ever think you're punishing me because you ask me to fuck you."

My Killian. He always knew what to say to melt my heart.

We moved me from the couch to the bed and we didn't come out of the room until the next morning.

I woke up in Killian's arms. They tightened.

"You're awake?" he asked.

"Yes." I nuzzled his shoulder.

"I have something to show you." He stood up, took a t-shirt from his drawer, and put it over my head.

"This can't wait?"

"No." I watched him step into a pair of sweatpants and slip something small in his pocket.

He took my hand and guided me to the front door.

"I can't go outside like this. I'm not wearing panties and its broad daylight."

"My shirt is long enough." He hit a switch by the front door. "Close your eyes."

"If anyone is out front, I promise you will have blue balls for a month."

"My balls are safe," he said with sexy, low laughter.

I closed my eyes and let him lead me outside. I heard water but wasn't sure where it came from.

"Don't open them."

It was cold outside and the grass was freezing against my feet as he walked me onto his lawn. The first sprinkles I felt were strangely warm and then more poured down on top of me, plastering my shirt to my body.

"Open your eyes, Rebecca."

I did. I was standing in a circle of sprinklers that were spraying warm water. It made no sense.

"This is when I knew I loved you. That night we made love in the rain. After I returned from the hospital I had new sprinklers put in for just this spot. They emit cold or warm water depending on the season."

He couldn't see my tears with the water running over my face. I had no words, but he did. He went to his knee and pulled a ring from his pocket.

"Rebecca Lesley Cavanaugh will you marry me?"

Sobs burst from my throat and I fell to my knees. Killian's arms wrapped around me.

"Yes, yes, yes."

He hugged me a moment longer, then shifted back and took my hand. The ring fit perfectly.

"I love you," he said so beautifully.

"I love you and you're crazy. No one has hot and cold-water sprinklers put in their yard."

He laughed. "Then they haven't had sex in the rain."

"Not in broad daylight."

"We'll come back out here tonight." His wet lips came down on mine.

My Killian MacGregor, the romantic.

Chapter Thirty-Seven

I QUALIFIED FOR NATIONALS and took sixth place. No grumpy loser behavior for me. After my college graduation, I became Rebecca MacGregor.

Amanda, Malory, and my sister Candi were my bridesmaids. My sister and I reached an uneasy peace that improved each time I confronted her and wouldn't let her talk down to me. Lyle, Blitz, and Stump stood with Killian. Michael was our ring bearer.

For our honeymoon, we flew to a private island in the Caribbean that Killian rented.

Exhaustion had settled deep into my bones by the time we arrived. Soft-colored lights surrounded the covered patio. Killian lifted me into his arms and carried me over the threshold. He started undressing me as soon as we were inside.

"I know you're tired, but I want to soak in the Jacuzzi so we don't wake up sore from traveling."

The built-in Jacuzzi was adjacent to the ocean. We didn't wear suits, just stepped in and sank into the warm, refreshing water. Killian's arms circled my waist and pulled my back against his chest. He massaged my arms and shoulders before moving down to my thighs. He worked my muscles and I relaxed into his embrace, loving the smell of the ocean tempered by the scent of my husband. He finally rested his hands on my hips and kept them there.

"You're really not going to go any farther?" I asked with a yawn.

"Hmm, you're tired. I think I did a fairly good job of fucking my wife last night and I can hold out until the morning."

I turned around and kissed his neck. "Who asked you anyway? It's my turn to fuck you, husband."

"God, I love when you talk dirty."

I sank my teeth into his skin and felt him tense beneath me. Killian was right, fucking and making love were only semantics. Being loved was the key.

Three years later…

"Here, sweetie, take this to your father." I patted the two-year-old diapered bottom as he ran down the hall looking for Killian.

I heard the squeal of laughter a moment later and knew Mikey found his dad. I pulled the number twenty jersey over my head, grabbed my purse, diaper, everything bag and walked into the living room.

Killian placed Mikey's feet on the floor and gave me a look.

I crossed my arms. "It's your turn. What can I say?"

"It's always my turn when he's stinky."

"Poor baby," I said with an evil grin.

"I never get any respect on game day."

"Nope, but I'll take one of your diaper turns if you win."

"Hmm, what else do I get if I win?"

"This woman might surprise you." I gave him a suggestive eyebrow raise.

"It's a deal."

He pulled a plastic changing pad from the cabinet along with baby wipes. It amazed me how one child could take over a home so quickly. Every cabinet and drawer now had something baby related.

"Have you spoken to my mother?" Killian asked as he set to work.

"Yes, Michael's feeling better. I think he can come to next week's game."

The past year had been rough on Michael, and he'd spent weeks in the hospital. We valued every day we had with him and I truly hoped he lived long enough for his namesake to remember him. I patted my small, rounded belly. I didn't know if this next one would get the chance to know his or her uncle.

"You okay?" Killian asked from where he sat on the floor.

"Yes, I'm doing wonderful." I smiled.

"Dada, ball," Mikey said.

"Yes, buddy, Daddy's playing ball today and you're coming to the game." Killian finished his brilliant diapering skills and tickled his son.

No more of Killian's bad behavior on game days. Killian tried and managed a little better after we married, but the real change happened when his son was born. He entered his playing zone with smiles and laughter. He saved his intensity for the locker room. He remained moody when he lost a game, but the year before, the day before Mikey's first birthday, the Scorpions won the Super Bowl.

"Up you go, Bud. I'll see you and Mommy at the stadium."

Killian handed him over and Mikey started crying.

"He's such a Daddy's boy. Maybe the next one will be a girl and she'll cry when I leave," I muttered but couldn't help my smile.

"I cry when you leave." Killian pulled me and Mikey in close, kissed me quickly on the lips and his son on the head.

"Good luck."

"Thanks, but I already have all the luck I need." He picked up his bag and walked out.

I squeezed my son's sweet body close. "Come on. Let's brush your teeth and get you dressed so we can go see your daddy play."

That night I slipped into the purple and black number twenty, baby doll nightie I discovered online. It cracked me up because I just couldn't see another man wanting his wife or girlfriend wearing it.

Killian walked in talking, "He's asleep." Silence. "Fuck."

I turned slowly so he got the full effect.

"You are one hot momma."

"I'm your hot momma."

"Come here. It's a shame to take this off, so we'll leave it on for a while."

"Whatever the star quarterback wants," I said saucily.

"The star quarterback wants his wife screaming." His hands cupped my ass and pulled me close, taking my mouth at the same time.

After the kiss ended, he placed kisses over my neck and exposed collarbone.

"Fuck me, Killian."

"My pleasure."

For maybe the millionth time, my husband made me scream.

The End

There is another football book that includes Killian though he and Rebecca are not the main story. It's titled GOAL, book II in the Completion Sports series. For more information on me and my books, visit wickedstorytelling.com.

Holly

About Holly

Holly S Roberts is an award-winning author which includes appearing on the USA TODAY list multiple times and selling more than one million books worldwide. Max, her Rottweiler, is never far from her side because he listens when she has plot problems and offers rare insights when encouraged with cookies.